Blocked

JOANNA INNES

RSE Publishing

Laurens, South Carolina

Copyright © 2015 by Joanna Innes

ISBN 978-1518897511

Printed in the United States of America
Edited by Amanda L. Capps
Book Design by Michael Seymour
Cover Design by Dan Fowler

PUBLISHER'S NOTE

Without limiting the rights under copyright reserved above, no part of this publication may be reproduced, stored or transmitted in any form, or by any means without the prior written permission of the copyright owner.

The scanning, uploading, distribution of this book via the internet or any other means without the permission of the copyright holder is illegal and punishable by law. Please purchase only authorized editions and do not participate in or encourage piracy of copyrighted materials. Your support of the author's rights is appreciated.

Cover Art

The cover includes a painting by
Mary Walker of Charleston, South Carolina

The Muse

Lydia Drexel paced around her studio. Her canvas remained blank, its white surface demanding a response. For the first time in her life, she felt her muse had deserted her.

Always before, a collection of ideas pushed at her, waiting to be chosen. She had met each new day in the studio with energy and confidence. But now something was wrong. Despite the good reviews and sales for her solo show, her inner self could not find satisfaction.

She thought back to her father's words of warning when she was still in high school. "You want to be an artist? Well then, my advice is to find a rich husband." She'd laughed at the time, confident enough about herself and her art that no one could have dampened her spirits, not even her well-meaning father.

Now she was sleepless, frustrated, and sad.

"I don't want to be all dried up, a mere husk of an artist, painting the same painting over and over in slightly new shapes and colors."

She flopped down in a rocker that she kept in one corner of the studio for relaxing and stared at her current canvas on the easel.

"If I can't be a painter, I'll move on. Find a new career. I can't continue like this."

She pulled her fingers through her dark curls in a few swift movements and then stood and pushed on around the room again, examining each of the paintings from her most recent show.

She stopped in front of a favorite painting, one that had come to her in a flash. It had been one of those rare times when the composition of the painting formed itself in a single session. It had felt effortless, even magical. But would she still value the painting in six months? It was eerie the way a painting that felt complete and satisfying at the time of creation could later seem unfinished, lacking in some major way, even doomed for the trash pile.

She remembered how this painting's title came to her late one sleepless night. Standing in front of the painting now, she spoke its title softly, "Self Contained." Although she sometimes changed titles, she believed this title to be timeless.

Splashes of vivid color filled the outer rim of the canvas and swirled in a mixture of darkening tones toward a vortex while tiny thread-like shafts of light in pale colors crisscrossed the entire painting. The crisscrosses held the colors in place in a feathery fashion like an open-air cage, an aviary.

At the show, one of her students had asked her about the title.

"Dr. Drexel, I'm curious about the title for this painting."

Normally Lydia might have been annoyed. She believed it was the viewer's job to find meaning in a painting, and she did not like to be questioned about her intentions. Either the painting had something to say, or it didn't. It should not need an explanation. But she sensed the student had a genuine curiosity. "What did you want to ask me, Anne?"

"I wondered how you chose the title, if it had any additional meaning." Anne paused, as if uncertain whether she should continue.

Lydia smiled, thinking of herself at that young age. "I'd rather hear what you think the title means."

Anne looked again at the painting. "Perhaps the crisscrossing lines are holding the colors in place—containing them, but that seems too literal."

"Good. What else?"

"I guess it depends on what the artist means by what is hidden behind the lines." She paused. "Maybe whatever the artist is thinking is being held in check. In a prison—but the lines are too delicate to be a prison."

Lydia was pleased that her student had said "the artist" instead of "you." She thought it so tactful.

After a moment, Anne continued. "I think the artist is experiencing some kind of struggle. Perhaps it's something very personal, and the crisscrossing lines keep both the viewer and the artist from getting too close to the secret."

"Well done."

"You mean I actually have it right?"

"I'm not going to say anything about right or wrong, just that I'm pleased you made the effort to look closely for meaning. It's a compliment to the artist, Anne, that you are willing to put forth the effort."

☙

Looking at the painting now, Lydia decided her student had made a good point. In some way, the painting could be connected to the blockage she was experiencing.

"Now it's my problem to discover the secret, to pull away the bars, to find a new direction for my work."

To ease her troubles, Lydia invited Charles, her mentor and friend at the college, for a drink on her deck that evening. Years ago, he took her under his wing when she was new in the department; he had been there long enough to earn tenure and to be revered. He pointed out what she needed to do to get tenure, told her whom to avoid and whom to watch, and guided her toward success. And always, he treated her as someone special. She had found him attractive and entertaining and thought for a while that she might become his muse. He didn't say, and she didn't ask about his preferences, but she most certainly knew that a friendship like this, where sex wasn't an issue, offered a special kind of security. It freed her to be more open with him and less questioning of his intentions. She could argue with him, laugh or cry with him, and never feel she had to hide anything from him.

Charles arrived looking refreshed and ready for a challenge. She told him she felt as vacant as a blank canvas.

"What you need is a vacation." Charles leaned back in the deck chair and crossed one expensively shod foot over the other; his long legs extended to the edge of the deck, and his back stretched into a lazy loop. He ran his hand through his thinning white hair and sighed. "A change of scenery. New people and new places will bring fresh ideas."

She didn't want to hear these well-meaning suggestions.

"Charles, you want to solve every problem with a vacation." She moved from her perch on the deck railing to a chair beside Charles.

Charles turned to face Lydia. "And what, my dear, is wrong with that?"

"It's irresponsible. Nothing is solved by running away."

"Running away, that's all that you see?" Charles reached for Lydia's hand, turned the palm up, and traced his forefinger along the lifeline. "I see a tall, dark stranger in your future. He will solve all your problems, Lyd, if you let him."

She scoffed. "Of course! Let me guess. He'll set me up in a studio in SoHo, find me an agent, and in six months, I'll become famous."

"So sarcastic this evening. Are you going to tell me the trouble?"

"If only I could."

Charles sipped his drink and waited.

"I think if I could understand what's wrong with this last set of paintings,

I could move ahead."

"But the show sold more than usual, and you had good reviews. Are you telling me you're uncomfortable with success?"

She stood and walked around the deck a couple of times before sitting down again beside Charles. "I know it all looks good on the surface, but underneath there's a problem. A weakness I can't define."

"And you want me to find it?"

"No, silly. I just want to talk about it."

"Ah, talk away, then."

"But I have nothing to say."

Charles picked up Lydia's empty glass. "Then let's try another method."

Lydia looked at the rolling hills that spread and rose toward the mountains while she waited for Charles to return from the kitchen. The rising purple shapes in the distance formed a soothing line of demarcation, a peaceful image—one she had used many times in her landscape paintings, both in realistic and abstract ones. But the view provided only a small measure of peace now. In this state of mind, she could perceive it almost as a cliché.

"Here you go," Charles said as he handed Lydia the glass of wine.

"Thanks. Nice to have someone wait on me."

"Um, could it become a habit? Are you saying you're lonely?"

"No. But I guess you'd have to say I'm at that precarious age." She knew many of her friends thought she should be searching for a mate, "for company," they often added, as if she were beyond the years for love and romance. Funny how one continues to feel so young, despite the years. Even though she'd given up looking for romance, she never thought of it as an impossibility. Perhaps her shining knight would yet appear. And if not, she had continued to believe that it did not matter; her life was full, focused on her art.

"Certainly, many have tried their games of matchmaking for me."

"May I say that I've never noticed any efforts on your part to snare a man?"

"Snare? A peculiar choice of words, Charles."

"Is it?"

Lydia was silent for a moment. "Well, I suppose, to be perfectly honest, I resent the idea that I would have to snare a man."

"Put in that light, I can see your objection. But we both know you're attractive and desirable, so there is no need for you to take offense by the word."

"I knew there was a good reason for inviting you over, Charles. You know just the right thing to say."

"Lydia, listen. I really do think you should take a few weeks away from the studio. Just a short journey. Something different. Not hours of gallery hopping and museum camping. Perhaps my cousin's cottage for a couple of weeks. A stack of books and a case of wine. How does that sound?"

"I'll think about it, Charles."

Mountain Retreat

Charles contacted his cousin George Randolph and his wife Ruth in the nearby Blue Ridge Mountains and made arrangements for Lydia to spend two weeks in their rental cabin. Lydia packed the books and several bottles of wine, just as Charles had suggested. Against his suggestion, she also packed a couple of her favorite sketchbooks and some watercolors.

After she'd unpacked and settled into a rocker on the front porch, she phoned Charles. "I hope this doesn't end up being a nightmare. If I get stuck in the doldrums, will you promise to come to my rescue?"

"Always delighted to rescue you, my dear."

"Actually, it's perfectly beautiful here. I love this little front porch with its rockers. I'm sitting here now with my feet propped up on the railing."

"Enjoying a glass of wine, I hope."

"Indeed."

"You found everything in good order, then?"

"Perfect. Right down to the stacks of puzzles and magazines. I have several *New Yorkers* here beside me. Most of the jokes are classics, so who cares if they're back issues? And I'll read the fiction, even though half the time, these new authors have crazy endings. Modern writing. Ech!"

"What's this? Castigating aspersion on modern ways? What does art history tell us about new trends?"

"Don't start. You know perfectly well that I accept the most important trends in modern art."

"Literature is a sister art, is it not?"

"I see you want to pick an argument, but I'm too lazy and too comfortable to engage."

"Argument? I think *discussion* is the word."

"You're right, but for now I just want to be a glob of inertia."

Charles laughed. "That you will never be, but go ahead and relax. I'm glad to see that Cousin George has pleased you."

"And how does he do that? Did you tell him what I like?"

"Perhaps. A hint or two."

"Oh Charles, you really are too good to me."

"Just remember that when I call on you for a favor."

"A favor? Is something brewing? Something of note on campus?"

"My lips are sealed."

"You're going to tease me like this? Now that I'm up here away from everything and everybody? Not fair!"

Charles burst into laughter and then paused significantly to heighten the moment. "Well, it's nothing terribly stupendous."

"Come on. Give!"

"Oh, all right. The new dean has sent out an official letter. You'll have it in your box when you return."

"A letter. Not e-mail?"

"Yes, *tres* official, you see."

"And?"

"He's offering sabbaticals to those of us who are in our final quarter, and that's me, as if we could forget. But I'll need supportive letters of recommendation. I can count on you? We can call it our collaborative effort."

"Is that all? I thought there might be some scandal. Something to kick some life into that dull campus."

"Surely you aren't saying that a sabbatical is nothing."

"Obviously, it's something for you. How about me?"

"You'll have your turn. You're years away from retirement."

"They may never offer them again. The way the budget gets hacked and yanked around, it's not as if we can count on much of anything."

"True, but we did finally get a cost of living raise."

"After three years of going without!"

"So that makes the sabbatical a rarity, after all. Just promise me you'll say my project is divine and that the department will benefit exponentially."

She silently upbraided herself for her lack of generosity. "Of course, I'll help, but honestly, I don't think you need it."

"Ah, but I do. And now I'm off to do some pavement pounding and politicking, dear Lydia. I'll need a few more people in my pocket to seal the deal. Such is the way of academe."

"Yes, that relentless part of the job, all that slipping in and out of people's pockets. You're made for it, but not me. I wouldn't care if I never had to go to another faculty meeting or serve on another committee."

"There, there, my dear. Just have another glass of wine and enjoy the view for me. *Au revoir.*"

Lydia pocketed her cell phone and selected a copy of *The New Yorker*, but after scanning an article, she put it aside. She couldn't concentrate. The invisible monster, as she had begun to call it, gripped her again and wouldn't let go. A chill ran down her spine. *What is happening to me?*

She wanted to drink in the beauty of the mountains, to find solace in the layers of shapes and colors that normally would sooth her mind, but she felt only confusion and abandonment. Almost without thought, she picked up her sketchbook and began to pencil the scene, thinking at least this one activity—this engrained habit—could bring distraction from her trouble.

With her eyes and mind focused on the task before her, she was not aware of the figure approaching. The voice startled her.

"Hello there," the tall young woman called from the path that led to the cabin.

Lydia put her sketchbook down, rose from her chair, and leaned over the porch railing to get a better look at the person invading her space. She hadn't expected to see another soul for weeks.

"I'm your neighbor. I was just out for my walk, and I thought I'd come welcome you. Mr. Randolph told us you'd be here."

Lydia noted the young woman's hiking attire and the backpack thrown over one shoulder. "A neighbor? I wasn't aware of anyone living nearby."

"Well, you wouldn't know it, I guess, because of the forest. I took a short cut from our place through the woods. Actually, I'm out gathering some odds and ends for my work."

"For your work?"

"Yes, I use bits of twigs and grass and flowers and mosses and such to make things."

"What sort of things?"

"Just pretties I sell at the Farmer's Market."

"That sounds interesting. Please," Lydia said, "come up and sit for a while."

"Are you sure? I wouldn't want to bother you."

"Not at all. I'd like to hear more about your work." Lydia offered her hand to the wholesome looking young woman. "My name is Lydia Drexel."

"I'm Jan Johnson. I live with my brother on the old Swanson place."

Lydia knew that people who lived in the mountains often identified themselves in this way. Although she had no idea who the Swansons might be, probably she would find out eventually. She pointed to a rocker and took the other for herself. "You must be thirsty after your long walk. Would you like some wine?"

"Oh, no thanks. I don't drink. And I've got my water right here." She pulled a water bottle from her bag, causing Lydia to notice the young woman's graceful movements. She would make an excellent model for figure drawing.

"So tell me about your crafts, Jan."

"They're nothing much. I wouldn't even call them crafts. I just glue this stuff into some sort of picture like thing. Little scenes, you might say. Or sometimes I decorate the boxes my brother makes."

"I'd like to see them."

"You would? I guess you'd have to come to the Farmer's Market. We have it on the weekends down in the village."

"I could do that. And your brother makes boxes?"

"Yes, ma'am. At first, we made gifts for neighbors and friends, and then it just sort of spread from there."

"Interesting." Lydia thought the young woman might be falsely modest and found it an appealing attribute after her years of working with overly confident, often cocky students. She was curious now as to the history of this attractive person. "So you've lived here on the mountain for a long time?"

Jan began to rock slowly, and Lydia wondered if she were asking too many questions.

"I guess you'd say that. It seems like a long time. My brother and I continued to live here after our parents got killed in a car wreck a few years ago."

"Oh, my goodness. I'm so sorry." Lydia wanted to show her sympathy, but she wasn't sure how much to say. She paused for a few moments before changing the subject. "It's really beautiful up here. I came because I was having trouble with my artwork, and my friend suggested a vacation might help. I'm really glad I came."

Jan turned quickly toward Lydia. "You're an artist? What kind?"

BLOCKED

"I'm a painter, mostly. Occasionally I do some watercolors."

"Really! I've always wanted to be a real artist."

"Maybe you are."

"Not with my silly little things."

"But people like them enough to buy them, don't they?"

"Well, yeah, but that doesn't mean much of anything. They buy all kinds of stuff."

Lydia thought this comment showed a certain amount of intelligent discernment. It was true that people often bought without knowledge.

Their rockers moved quietly on the wood floor, creating a pleasing rhythm, and in the distance, a vehicle traveled up the winding road toward them.

Abruptly, Jan stood up. "That'll be my brother. That's his truck coming. He gets worried about me. Can't seem to see that I'm a grown woman."

Lydia noticed the annoyance in Jan's voice. "Well, we'll invite him to sit with us. I'd like to meet him."

"Oh, he'll be in a hurry, and he's not much for talking, so I don't think he'll want to stay."

Lydia thought Jan seemed nervous. Was she afraid of her brother?

The truck door slammed, and in a few minutes, a tall young man in jeans and a plaid shirt emerged from the woods and appeared on the path. He strode with confidence toward the porch.

"You didn't have to come looking for me, Bryce."

Lydia introduced herself before there could be a confrontation and invited Bryce to join them. "Come on up and sit with us." She motioned toward the rockers and took a spot on the wide porch rail for herself.

Bryce stood for a few moments before removing his ball cap, climbing the few steps and sitting down. Lydia could see he was uncomfortable. His posture was stiff and his brow was wrinkled. A handsome boy of probably no more than twenty. If he smiled, he could pass for a young James Dean.

"I've been hearing about Jan's crafts, and I'm curious about your boxes."

Bryce gave his sister a cross look. "You've been giving the whole family history?"

Jan shook her head, causing her long blonde ponytail to swing gently against her shoulders. "Miss Lydia is an artist, Bryce."

Bryce said nothing.

"I told her our stuff, well my stuff, isn't much. But your boxes are really special."

"Just something to do with the odd bits of wood around here." He stood up and motioned to his sister. "We'd better go." He turned toward Lydia. "We're on the old Swanson place, just through the woods about two miles. Number 26 is our mailbox when you drive along the road. Let us know if you need anything."

Jan said, "Maybe you'll come to the Market? It's Friday and Saturday from eight o'clock until about four."

"Yes, I think I will. And if you're out walking again, please stop for a visit."

"Thanks, I might do that."

Lydia watched the handsome couple walk down the path. What kind of relationship did they have? Jan must be the older of the two, but not by much, maybe a couple of years at most. What could their story be, left alone here after their parents' tragic death? Surely they had some income other than what they made from their craft sales. They had a vehicle and both wore expensive hiking boots and standard L.L. Bean clothing, she surmised, so they were not destitute. Perhaps an insurance policy provided income. Maybe Charles knows something more. She would ask the next time she talked with him.

Settled back into her rocker, she forced herself to resume her drawing, but the light was already changing, so that she had a quite different impression of the view. It had become sinister. *Or is that merely my state of mind?*

Another Visitor

The next morning, Lydia slept late. Charles would say, "See, I told you a little vacation would help." But would it help her find her muse again? That was the question.

Stretched out on her yoga mat, she breathed in deeply and expelled the air slowly. She thought about how so many media articles wanted to guide people toward success in all areas of life if they would only follow their suggestions, yoga being one. She believed it helped; coordinating activities for mind, body, and emotions certainly couldn't hurt. *Popular solutions. I need something more. Ideas. I want ideas.* She rubbed her brow with her fingertips to release the pressure.

A favorite pair of jeans, a cotton tee, but no shoes. Bare feet in the morning were part of her normal routine.

Glancing in the mirror on her way to the kitchen, she noticed that the puffiness under her eyes had lifted slightly. She turned one way and then the other, checking her figure. "You don't look half bad, considering your fifty-first birthday is in the wings. No, it's your brain that's in trouble, not your body."

While the coffee brewed, she stepped outside to see what the morning felt like. Pleasantly cool with a breeze ruffling the leaves.

"Sweater weather. Charles was right."

She thought Charles had come to know her well. It was both comforting and slightly annoying that he could predict her moods and behavior so successfully.

"Um, talking out loud to myself, must be the freedom of these mountains. Now if only it brings a new consciousness-raising."

She noticed how the sun was just beginning to filter through the trees on the backside of the cabin, and the birds were conversing at full tilt. She spotted a pair of bluebirds among the trees a few feet from the porch, streaks of brilliant blue zipping through the air. How thoughtful of Mr. Randolph to place birdhouses and feeders around the cabin. She decided to get extra birdseed when she went to the village.

"Maybe I can lure some special breeds." She had noticed the field glasses and a book on birds resting on the coffee table.

"I'd love to see an indigo bunting and some of the pretty warblers. Maybe some hummingbirds?" On one of the kitchen shelves, tucked back in a corner, a hummingbird feeder had not escaped her notice.

"Mr. Randolph must be a birder."

Lydia had settled down in her rocker with her first cup of the rich, dark Colombian coffee she loved and picked up the field glasses when she heard a motor in the distance. It didn't sound like Bryce's truck, more like a car. "So much for a quiet time in the mountains."

Anyone arriving in a vehicle had to park in the gravel slot provided and proceed on foot up the steep path leading to the cabin, which she noted, gave her time to prepare herself for a visitor. It wasn't long before Lydia heard the car door slam, followed by rhythmic crunching along the path. All the sounds up here seemed intensified. No road traffic, just the wind in the trees and the occasional scurrying of a small animal, if you listened carefully.

She was tempted to use the glasses for an advance peek at her visitor but didn't want to be caught snooping. Soon she could see that it was a tall man approaching slowly, as if he were burdened by stiff joints. As he came into full view, she knew it was George Randolph, the owner of the cabin. He was dressed as if he were going hunting, but he wasn't carrying a rifle.

Lydia stood up and walked down the steps to greet her landlord. "Good morning," she called.

"Mornin', ma'am."

"Lydia, please."

He paused for a moment, searched her face, and smiled. "And it's George, Lydia."

Lydia returned the smile. "I've got a pot of coffee. How about a cup?"

"Don't mind if I do. Sure hope I'm not disturbing you. Just wanted to check to see if everything was okay and if you needed anything."

Lydia pointed to a rocker and said, "Everything is fine. Cream or sugar?"

"Black will be fine."

She brought the steaming cups of coffee, handed one to her visitor, and sat down beside him. They sipped their coffee in silence. Usually she would have felt uncomfortable with this much silence with a stranger, but she thought the atmosphere almost demanded silence. Respect.

Finally, she said, "You have a good crop of bluebirds. They like the houses you've provided."

"I'm glad to see those lively little friends back here. We had a stretch when we hardly ever saw a bluebird. My wife Ruth and I have had a long fascination with the blue birds."

Another silence.

"I had another visitor yesterday," Lydia said.

"Oh? Someone local?"

"Yes, the young people who live on the old Swanson place, Jan and Bryce Johnson." She watched for a reaction but saw none.

"That's a bit curious. If you don't mind me asking, what did they want?"

"Jan was out walking and stopped to welcome me. She said you had told them that I would be here. Then later, Bryce came in his truck for his sister."

She watched George scratch his beard and she waited.

"Well now. I suppose I must have mentioned that you'd be here, probably when I saw them at the Market."

Another of those long pauses. Lydia thought it a bit strange for her landlord to take up residence on her porch like this. She wondered if it was his usual habit or if he were deciding what to tell or not to tell her. She hoped he would reveal something more about the brother and sister and their circumstances, perhaps even something about Bryce's temperament. She decided not to ask any more questions. Maybe she should let him enjoy his own property for a few minutes before he moved back into his usual routine. Certainly not every moment needed to be filled with talk. This, she decided again, was exactly the kind of place where talk seemed less important.

Eventually, toward the end of his coffee, George told her how the Johnson family had moved into the house a dozen years ago and had gradually renovated the old place, putting on an addition with lots of big windows to catch the view and a big wraparound porch with rockers for their visitors. And at just about the time it was completed, they were in the car wreck. Rumor said they had come from a party late at night and probably had been drinking. On one of the sharp curves coming up the mountain, Mr. Johnson lost control of the car, maybe trying to avoid hitting an animal, and it had turned over and over, falling to the bottom of the ravine, killing both his wife and him.

"What a terrible shock for everyone," Lydia said. "How old were the children when it happened?"

"Just teenagers. Still in high school. It hasn't been that long, maybe five or six years."

"And they stayed in the house?"

"I think they had no place to go. Someone told me they were both adopted. And anyway, I suspect they didn't want to leave their friends. Those last years of high school are usually precious times."

"But how did they manage?"

"People around here are generous. Everyone made sure they were okay. And the parents had a good life insurance policy, according to one of my lawyer friends."

"I wonder why they haven't gone to college, especially if they have the money, but maybe they fell into working with their art. Jan told me that she and Bryce sell their crafts at the Farmer's Market."

"That's right. They have a good business going. Of course, everyone wants to help them out, so they continue to buy. But it's good work. Original. The boxes Bryce makes are finely crafted, some of them cut into puzzles, beautifully sanded and finished. I own a few myself."

"I plan to go to the Market so I can see their work."

George rocked slowly and downed the last of his coffee. Lydia decided he must be preoccupied, concentrating on something beyond the moment. She thought about her next question carefully. It wouldn't do to create a problem.

"One other thing, George. I don't want to be out of line, but I'm wondering if you've noticed anything unusual about Bryce. His behavior, I mean. I thought he was overly concerned about his sister visiting me. It seemed odd, like a jealous husband."

George stood up and put his empty cup on the porch railing. He looked off toward the mountains and finally said quietly, "I'd better be going."

Lydia watched as he went down the steps and started down the path. But then he came back to make a circuit around the cabin. Lydia wondered what he was looking for, but she supposed it was his habit to check and double-check his property.

Right before he dropped out of view, he turned and called to Lydia. "I'll make sure these feeders are stocked so you can enjoy the birds." He took a few more steps away before turning again toward her. "We have some rare ones visiting us now and then."

"Rare ones visiting us now and then." Was that a subtle hint, a way of answering her question about Bryce without committing himself? How peculiar.

"Any more strange visitors and I'll have to change my main purpose here from sketching and resting to sleuthing."

The Market

Lydia decided to go to the Market early enough to see a good selection, especially the boxes George had mentioned. She would pick up a few veggies, too, for her meals this week. Fresh tomatoes, squash, corn—lovely to eat and wonderful subjects for a still life. She smiled. If she couldn't get an idea for a painting, at least she would have a tasty meal.

She felt a little twinge of excitement over arranging a still life and thought, *Maybe I'm moving past my block. But don't count on it. It's going to take more than a still life to get back to normal, whatever that is.*

As she walked down the steps and then onto the pine nettle-covered path, she noticed a bluebird perched on the birdhouse. "What a handsome fellow you are. Perhaps your mate is inside. Will there be babies soon? No wonder the Randolphs find you exciting."

Lydia possessed a longtime fascination with wildlife. It never failed to give her pleasure, surprising her at times with the intensity of feeling it spawned. She remembered admiring her mother's ability to mimic bird calls. While they worked in the garden together, through her mother's imitation, Lydia learned to identify many of the local birds: a cardinal, a bobwhite, a blue jay, and the rain dove, sounding so forlorn.

Often she found herself, now that her mother had been dead for a few years, wondering what it would be like to talk with her again. When she was a young child, they had spent hours working together. It had always been natural to share her feelings and her questions with her mother.

A moment of sadness passed through Lydia, but then she was in her car

BLOCKED

and starting down the mountain with new thoughts. She wondered again what she would find in the village and at the Market. It felt like a small but pleasing adventure.

Soon she was passing the almost hidden entrance to what must be the road leading to Jan and Bryce's house. But the driving on this steep, curving road demanded her full attention, so she could not discern much. A mailbox. Bryce had mentioned their mailbox. No time to check for a name or number. Even though she was early, she didn't expect to see them now. She knew they would have packed up earlier that morning to get to the Market to set up their display.

She hoped she would not be disappointed, but then, she chastised herself for being negative. So often, artwork that others valued could be a disappointment. Not the work in major museums, of course, but in a small mountain village, what could she expect? "Don't be a snob, Lydia."

Within another fifteen minutes, she was driving along the tree-lined Main Street. It gave her the feeling that she had been there before, but then, it was like a hundred other villages. Tidy houses, shops, the usual public buildings, tubs of bright red geraniums, and those colorful banners hanging from the lamp poles, Welcome to Hollyville. She spotted the market stalls lining the park next to the post office and turned into a side street looking for shade, but all of the parking was taken, so she drove up and down until she found a spot several blocks away. She didn't mind walking. It would give her a chance to examine this quaint little village more closely.

Already the morning sun was bearing down. Good thing she had brought a hat along. Wanting to look her best, she adjusted it at a jaunty angle and walked slowly toward the Market. White picket fences, porch swings, and beautifully planted flower gardens bordered freshly mowed lawns. Lots of pride displayed in Hollyville.

A large family must live in this rambling Victorian house. Four bikes of different sizes parked on the wraparound porch and a basketball hoop over the garage. Assorted smaller toys scattered in the lawn.

But no one seemed to be around. Everyone must be at the Market.

Lydia walked along Main Street, admiring the shops. The bookstore displayed in its large front window a collection of children's books and handmade toys, and the sign in the window announced the Children's Story Hour for that afternoon, *Charlotte's Web,* one of her favorites.

Several craft and gift shops caught her attention, but it would be better to stop on her way back from the Market. If she were disappointed with the crafts at the Market, she might find something to her liking in one of the shops. Some small gifts to take back to a few of her friends.

The first market stalls were devoted to local produce. Again, she noted the pride shown in the colorful arrangement of the vegetables, everything neatly lined up, almost picture perfect. It didn't take Lydia long to make her selections and to move on toward the crafts.

She found the usual assortment of crocheted and embroidered work, hand towels and tea towels with decorative edging. Birdhouses painted in muted shades. Carved wooden bowls and a variety of utensils, all functional and well-crafted. Patchwork quilts in a myriad of colors, bits of some family's past sewn into patterns. And a few tables devoted to flea market items. Someone's trash was another person's treasure. So far, nothing inspired her. She dismissed it as being what she had expected to find, only mildly interesting.

Lydia was surprised when Jan called her name. She looked up and saw her standing by her stall just a few feet away.

"I'm glad to see you made it, Miss Lydia."

Lydia noticed Jan's attire, a becoming cotton print tiered skirt and peasant blouse in hues of soft green that complemented her blonde hair and blue eyes, quite different from the hiking clothes she'd worn at their first meeting.

"How pretty you look, Jan."

"Thanks. I made this outfit myself."

"Lovely. You're good at sewing too."

"It fills the time."

"Are you here alone today? I don't see Bryce."

"Oh, he'll be back. He's gone to get us some snacks. I had something ready for us, but in our rush, I went off without it this morning."

Lydia began to examine Jan's crafts, and she saw that the girl was quite clever in the way she blended the basic materials. The bits of dried wildflowers and stems and grasses were woven artfully into small pictures. The frames were finely crafted.

"Did you make the frames too, Jan?"

"No, Bryce does them for me."

"He is a true craftsman."

"I knew you would think so. I'll let him show you his boxes. You'll like them even better."

Lydia noticed the pride in Jan's voice and concluded that whatever problem might exist between the two, it did not include jealousy.

A few moments later, Bryce arrived with bottles of soda and sandwiches.

"I've been admiring these frames you've made for Jan. They are quite fine, Bryce."

"They'll do."

"Will you show me your boxes?"

He moved down the row of stalls to his own.

Lydia was pleased indeed by the finely carved and finished boxes in their many different shapes and sizes, the wood grain shown in every case to its best advantage. She could only imagine the number of hours it took to select the wood and to decide the best way to use it. She held one of the boxes in her hand and lightly caressed its satiny finish.

"They are exquisite, Bryce."

"Thank you, ma'am."

"Have you tried marketing your work in other places?"

"Considered it."

"Good. I'm sure that these would do well in a crafts gallery in a major city."

"Others have said."

"Or you might consider selling online."

"That, too."

"But you are resistant, I believe."

"Somewhat. Don't really have to do it."

"Yes, I see. It would mean a different kind of approach, and it could become involved. That's a good point. I've never liked the problems that go with presenting and selling my work."

Lydia noticed that every few seconds, Bryce looked toward his sister's stall. Why was he so protective of her? And if he were that protective, why wasn't his stall placed beside hers so he could feel more comfortable? Probably she had resisted. It made good business sense. If people saw Bryce's work first, they would not be as interested in Jan's work. They may have agreed on this tact.

"I'd like to buy several of these."

"Okay, but I warn you. They're pricey."

"Do you have a price list?"

"No. Just tell me the ones you want."

It took a number of minutes to make her selection. Eventually, she pointed to four of them.

"That would be $200, ma'am."

"They are pricey, but they're worth it, Bryce."

She thought she saw a look of surprise in Bryce's face, but she couldn't be sure. Maybe it was a cynical look? She reached into her handbag for her checkbook and began to write the check, but Bryce said rather sharply, "Cash only, ma'am."

"Cash only, but my check is perfectly good."

"I have a policy. Cash only."

"A credit card, then? I don't have that amount of cash with me."

"No credit cards either. It's my policy."

"I should have realized. It would be easy to get a bad check." And perhaps he wanted to avoid the taxes. "I suppose I can go to the bank to get the cash for you."

"Bank closes at noon on Saturday during the summer, ma'am."

"I see. I'll have to pass on my purchase then. Maybe in the future, Bryce."

"Yes, ma'am."

She thought he was unusually stiff and sullen but realized that the boxes sold themselves. She smiled, thinking it was foolish to put him into a "box." She knew artists typically were a different species—hostile, in this case.

Mountain Hike

Lydia thought she was headed straight for the comfort of her cabin, but on the drive up the mountain, she suddenly changed her mind. It was a perfect day to explore a little of the land, so when she came to the Stone Mountain trailhead, she pulled into the parking area. She wasn't really dressed for a long hike, but she could at least get a little exercise, try just part of the trail, and perhaps get to the first lookout. The literature she'd read in the cabin noted several lookout points for this trail.

Fortunately, she had a pair of crosstrainers in the car, not as suitable as hiking boots, but they would have to do. In a few minutes, she had locked the car, secured her keys in her pocket, and was ready to climb.

The trail, well-maintained and worn from use, was easy to follow, steep but not too demanding for a person who exercised regularly. She knew how to pace herself, to take time to peruse the flora. The mountain laurel softly blanketed some of the out-croppings, and to the side of the trail, fine examples of wild azaleas added their delicate splash of color.

Lydia knew she would come for another Market visit, and she promised herself to have enough cash to buy at least one of Bryce's boxes. For now, though, she would let all of her questions about Bryce and Jan rest. Probably, she had let her imagination run to the wild side. Bryce and Jan had lived here a long time without incident, or at least as far as she knew. "Close it, Lydia, at least for now. Concentrate on the beauty of the earth."

She'd walked twenty minutes when she heard voices in the distance, probably hikers coming down the mountain, heading back to their vehicle.

The sounds carried so well, but not well enough for her to distinguish what was being said. A man and a young child? Or a young woman?

In another five minutes, she saw them on an upper level. She guessed they were close to the lookout, and that they would be resting and admiring the view. Somewhat winded, she would be glad to reach a resting spot. She slowed, giving the hikers time to finish their rest, preferring to be alone right now—for no particular reason—but maybe to remember this experience on the mountain as exclusively hers.

By the time she arrived, they were just preparing to move on. They had been sitting on a large boulder beside the guard rail.

"Fantastic view today," the man said.

Lydia noticed his wild and abundant curly grey hair and his unusually blue eyes. Kind eyes.

"This is my nephew. His first time hiking. We're having a day of it. And you? Just starting?"

"I'm out here on a whim. Otherwise, I guess I would be better prepared." Lydia glanced down at her feet.

"Ah, yes, hiking boots would serve you better. You probably could use some water too." He poured a cup from a thermos and handed it to her.

"Thank you. This is exactly what I need. Should have planned, but I thought I'd just try the trail for a bit, but then I couldn't stop. I wanted to reach this lookout. And it was worth it—just look at this view! We can see for miles."

All three of them paused, as if absorbing the time and the place, letting daily baggage drop away, a kind of reverence settling over them.

Lydia wiped at a tear. "This view is making me sentimental,"

"Nothing wrong with sentiment, and definitely nothing wrong with expressing it."

Another long pause. Then Lydia stood and stretched. "I'd better get moving, or I might never leave this spot."

"We're returning now, and if you'd like, come along with us. We can watch out for you. Right, Josh?"

"Yes, ma'am, we sure can."

What nice manners in this young boy. Curly hair must run in the family. She wanted to reach out and run her hand though Josh's rich red curls, but she thought it might bother him. At this in-between age, she guessed eleven or twelve, any touch of familiarity could be embarrassing for him.

"I'd like that," Lydia said. "Do you come here often?"

"A fair amount, several times a year here and on other trails. I live not too far away on the other side of the mountain. Came to this area after my wife died a few years ago. At first it was just to get away, but then I found I wanted to stay. I rented a place for a while, and now I'm building a place. I'll retire soon, and then I can be here year-round."

"I'm sorry for your loss, but glad you've found a place you like so much." Lydia noticed how easily he talked, as if he had nothing to hide.

"You aren't from here, I'd guess."

"No. Just taking a summer break. I'm a painter and a teacher."

"An artist, eh? Well, if you like landscape material, I'd say you've found your subject right here."

"It is perfectly beautiful and inspiring. I hope this time away will help me get back on track. I've been blocked recently."

"I see, well, best not to rush it. Just relax, is my advice, but then I don't suppose you're looking for advice." His laugh was rich and refreshing as a mountain stream.

Josh interrupted. "Uncle John, I'm going to go ahead. Okay?"

"Right, Josh, but take some care, lad. Don't want any broken bones. We don't climb out on these rocks without proper gear in place and your uncle nearby."

"Yes, sir. I know."

A few moments later, Lydia said, "What a handsome boy. I had to resist running my hands through those beautiful red curls."

"Handsome and a good boy too. Almost too good, but then there's time left for bedevilment, I suppose."

Lydia saw the smile spread over his face and into his eyes. Those kind eyes.

"Is he visiting you?"

"I have him for the weekend. My brother's boy. One of those modern wrecked marriages. My brother is divorced and gets the boy alternate weekends, but he had a job he couldn't leave this time."

"I was wondering if curly hair ran in the family."

Another burst of John's laughter.

"That's a wonderful laugh you have, John. I suppose I may call you John. I'm Lydia Drexel."

"Pleased to meet you, Lydia. I'm John Crawford."

Lydia inched her way down a particularly steep spot and knew her knees were not what they used to be.

John had gone ahead, but he stopped and reached back to offer a hand to Lydia.

"Those shoes aren't giving you enough traction."

"Right. Next time I'll be prepared."

"When might that be?"

"I don't know. I hadn't thought about it. I'm just getting settled in at the cabin I'm renting."

"Does that mean that my offer for a hike would be declined?"

"I don't know. Maybe." She paused. Lydia knew she must sound like an adolescent school girl, all befuddled, but it was such a surprise.

"It's supposed to be good weather the next few days, so name your day."

"Maybe I should give my old bones a rest. Today's Saturday? How about Monday?"

"Monday it is."

☙

The sun would soon be setting. The last rays were slicing low through the trees. That special quiet time of dusk approached.

Resting in a rocker, her feet on the railing and her hands cradling a mug of hot tea, Lydia reviewed her feelings. Strange, how she jumped from one frame of mind to another recently, but especially since her arrival there. Charles would tease her, no doubt, saying she was relaxing for once in her life, instead of sticking to a rigid schedule. "He knows me well. I'm lucky to have such a good friend for all these years."

She picked up her sketchbook and turned the pages slowly until she came to one that pleased her. It revealed the feeling she had for this quiet place, but it lacked something. Edge. To most viewers, she believed, it would be a simple rendering of a mountain scene. She hadn't intended it to be anything more than a record of her time here, so why attach more significance to it? Yet, it held her attention, and she believed that was a good thing, a signal that perhaps she was moving beyond whatever had held her in check previously.

Her mind traveled back to the conversation she'd had with her student about one of her paintings. Interesting how Anne had intuited so much, suggesting that it showed the painter's struggle to uncover some kind of secret. "If I pulled those strands of color away from the painting, what would I have left?"

Lydia leaned forward and listened carefully. Was that someone approaching? She thought she heard the sounds of movement in the woods. She stood up and listened again more intently. Definitely, someone was coming.

"Hello. Who's there?"

"Just me, Miss Lydia. Jan Johnson. I've brought you something."

Lydia wondered why Jan would be out at this late hour when the sun was setting. Surely it would be easy to get lost in these woods at night, or during the day, for that matter.

Jan came to the foot of the porch.

"Come on up. I'll get you some hot tea. I was just having a cup myself."

"Thanks, but I really have to get back."

"Right, it'll soon be dark. I wouldn't want to be in these woods at night."

"You forget that I know this area completely after living here for so long, and I brought a torch with me, so don't worry. But here, I brought you this." She offered a small package to Lydia.

"Come on, sit with me for a little while, Jan. If needed, I can give you a ride home."

"Well, just for a minute."

"Let's see what you have." Lydia untied the brown ribbon and pulled away the brown paper. "Oh, my goodness! It's so beautiful. One of Bryce's boxes." Lydia turned it in her hands and stroked its satin surface. "But I'm mystified."

"Bryce wanted you to have it. He said that you being an artist and all made a difference. That if you admired his work, knowing art the way you do, it meant something special. That the money doesn't matter."

Lydia felt tears forming and for a moment couldn't speak.

"I'm quite overwhelmed. This is such a beautiful gift."

BLOCKED

"I'm glad you're pleased. I knew you would be."

"I had already decided that when I come back to the Market, I would bring enough cash to buy a few of them."

"Oh, you're coming back?"

"I want to, yes."

Confusion

Lydia stayed on the porch until the light faded and the dramatic drop in temperature with a chilling breeze forced her inside. It was almost cold enough to build a fire, but she chose instead a scarf for her neck and a heavier sweater. *A fire could be romantic, if I had someone to share it with.*

With a cup of spiced tea, she settled into one corner of the small couch, slipped off her shoes, and pulled the throw across her legs. She tried to convince herself that it felt good to be alone in this cozy spot. *If you committed yourself to someone, complications could take over your life—schedules to blend, disagreements to settle, and someone else's problems to consider. Who needs it?*

From time to time, this speech ran through her mind, as if she were afraid of a commitment, but more than that, she used it to keep her desires quiet. She longed for companionship and someone to cherish. She wasn't a selfish person, merely a cautious one. After so many years alone, it was understandable. She had watched people struggle through their broken relationships and had helped a close friend survive a messy divorce. Avoiding that kind of pain made good sense, yet if she could find the right person, she knew she would take the risk of marriage and a settled life.

Her thoughts turned back to her art, her deepest concern—this new struggle with her muse. She found herself questioning even her choice as a painter. Would life as a craftsman have been better than that of a painter? They didn't seem to yearn for ideas and stimulation. They just went out back, cut down a tree and made something different, something useful from it. Typically, those who practiced the fine arts looked down on "crafts," but she realized that was the type of narrow-minded thinking that her professorial peers used to justify their intolerance.

She reached for Bryce's box and admired again the beautiful wood grain and satin finish. Bryce and Jan enjoyed a simple life. Apparently, they weren't bothered by what they should do next, whether their art was moving forward, or whether it made a statement.

She opened the box and saw for the first time a small square of folded paper. She was surprised that she hadn't seen it before, but reasoned that at dusk, the light had not been adequate, and the paper was tan, the same color as the wooden box. She unfolded the square carefully and saw what appeared to be some smudged writing. Was it letters or numbers? The thin, well-worn paper must have been folded and unfolded many times. Tiny tares formed in the creases.

What she needed was a magnifying glass or at least some better light. She moved to the best table lamp and turned it to its highest setting, but she still could not decipher what she was seeing. After more study, turning the paper one way and another, she thought she saw two numbers, a 5 or a 3 and a 1 or 7 could be 51 or 37 or other combinations, and what might be the letters A or P and N or M? Someone's initials? The numbers could be a year or a box number or a lock combination or any number of things. Finally, she refolded it, placed it back in the box, and returned the box to the coffee table. But her mind could not rest.

Surely, placing the paper in the box must have been a deliberate act. The paper may have no significance at all for her, but for someone, it must have importance.

She walked around the room thinking of the possibilities. Was it Jan or Bryce who had put the piece of paper in the box? If it were Jan intending to leave a message, wouldn't she have said something when she delivered the box? It had to be Bryce, but when and why? Something he left there for safekeeping but had forgotten? Again, she examined the note with her high-powered flashlight to study the smudges. When she squinted and held the message away, she thought she detected an image. Perhaps it wasn't a written message, after all, but a drawing.

Now her imagination worked in triple-time. She turned the paper this way and that to discover a literal meaning, but none came to her. Turned one way, it was a smudged waterfall with trees falling across it, another way a complicated bridge. In yet another way, the folds in the paper suggested to her a muted image of her painting, the one the student had talked about and questioned. She laughed at herself. *You're out on a shaky limb, girl.*

She poured herself a glass of wine and set a pot of water to boil for pasta, before returning to her spot on the couch. *If I drink enough, maybe I'll solve my problems.* She knew better, but she felt like being a little wild, for a change. She laughed, knowing what Charles would say. "Go for it, Lydia."

The most pressing question continued to nag her. Was it a message for her, or was it an accident, something left in the box inadvertently? She must find a way to ask Jan or Bryce about it.

After dinner, she decided to call Charles. He would be interested in this new mystery. She heard the stress in his voice immediately.

"Is something wrong?"

"I'm not doing so well with my proposal. It's that mealy-mouthed chair of our department. He can't seem to make up his mind. At first he was totally enthusiastic when I ran my plans by him, and then when I saw him a second time, he gave me that absent-minded, can't-be-bothered attitude of his."

"But Charles, you know Simpson does that at the drop of a hat. He probably just had something else on his mind and tuned you out."

"Exactly. And I don't want to be tuned out. It makes me fear that I won't get the sabbatical, and I have my heart set on it. I'm going to need your help as soon as you get back. You aren't coming back early, by chance?"

"No, I'm planning to finish out the month as planned, and I think I'll book the cabin for the rest of the summer."

"Don't tell me you're becoming part of that drab little community."

"Little, yes, but drab, no, Charles." She paused. "I met a very nice man today, and we're going for a hike Monday."

"Ah, this could be *interesting* for you, but do you think that's a good idea? Going for a hike with a stranger in the woods away from everything and everybody? This doesn't sound like you at all."

"Oh, honestly, Charles. It's a public trail."

"That doesn't mean there'll be somebody to help you if this guy decides to kidnap or kill you."

"Mr. Melodrama, you've obviously been watching too many thrillers. Now, back to your proposal. I'll be glad to look at it. You could e-mail it to me."

"It's your holiday. You shouldn't spoil it with work."

She could hear the resignation in his voice. For just a moment, she considered suggesting he could bring his proposal and they would work on it, but she decided it could wait a while. She needed to free herself from being such a people pleaser and from the mind-numbing institutional politics that Charles seemed to love.

Charles broke into her thoughts. "Any other news, besides a new lover?"

She laughed and took a sip of wine before telling Charles about the mysterious siblings, pinned at the hip and mired in psychological mystery, a modern, twisted version of the Bobbsey Twins. She explained her concern about Bryce's unusual treatment of his sister and the box with its message.

"Sounds like you're letting your imagination get the better of you, Lydie. A little advice, don't get too involved."

"That's rich. You send me up here for a vacation, a chance to clear my mind, and now you're telling me to seal myself up in this cabin."

"Whoa. What brought that on?"

She cleared her voice and waited. "I suppose I wanted you to be interested—to help me. After all, that's what you've done for me all these years."

"Ah, yes, but there are times when even the Great Charles fails, dear girl."

Lydia laughed.

"That's better."

"At least these distractions keep me from worrying so much."

"As long as you don't get too involved with your little mysteries, I'd say you are on the right path. You'll return refreshed and ready to help me with my worries."

"Back to the sabbatical proposal, I see."

"Of course. You don't expect me to be totally magnanimous, surely."

The Hike

This time, she was prepared. Dressed in layers with a protective hat and her hiking boots, she pocketed her charged cell phone and locked the cabin before walking down the steep path to her car. They had agreed to meet at the trailhead at 10:00 a.m. Her watch indicated she had plenty of time, actually extra time. She allowed herself to admit that she was eager to be with John.

As she drove by Jan and Bryce's mailbox, she wondered again how she might arrange a meeting with them. Maybe she would just drop in for a visit. After all, they had visited her without an invitation. Tomorrow, she could drive down to their house.

She pulled into the parking lot beside John's Subaru. He stood at the edge of the trail, one foot propped up on a large boulder, adjusting his shoelaces.

"You're early, according to my watch," Lydia said, as she approached him.

"And so are you." John finished tying his shoelace and turned toward Lydia.

Lydia again noticed his remarkable eyes.

"Are you an early riser?" she asked.

"No, just eager."

She noticed his tone of voice and smile and wondered if she should flirt back but decided she wanted to know more about him. *Gotta take this slow.*

"It's a fine morning for our explorations. I know some of the history of the area if you're interested," John said.

She thought he must have noticed her reluctance and was following her lead, which earned him a point.

"I know a little, but I expect to find some surprises."

"From me or the area?"

"Both, probably."

"You like surprises?"

"Love them, especially good ones."

John laughed. "I'll try to make mine good ones then."

They climbed for a while in silence, each pointing to a sight for the other to admire—a partially hidden blossom, a patch of soft moss, a bird in flight. She felt comfortable in the silence, which she interpreted as a good sign.

Some fifteen minutes into their hike, she asked, "Ready for some water?"

"Yes and a moment to talk. I've wanted to ask you about your work. Do you mind?"

"No, of course not, but I warn you that it's always better to see an artist's work than to listen to a description, especially from the artist."

"Is that a philosophical point of view, or are you shy when it comes to talking about your own work?"

She thought for a moment before answering. *He uses such a direct approach, but I think I like it—a welcome departure from what I hear at the college day in and day out.*

"I'm trying to decide how to answer you. I suppose it may be some of both. Most artists, I think, would prefer not to have to discuss their work, unless of course it is for a famous reporter." She laughed.

"Ah, can't fulfill that wish, I'm afraid, but perhaps you've already had that experience?"

"No, I was just joshing, but to be truthful, I may be feeling a little shy about telling you much about my work."

John seemed to wait for Lydia to continue. She noticed and thought it was especially considerate.

"So I guess I'd say my work is a mixture, sometimes figurative and realistic but other times abstract. I don't know if that's the sort of thing you want to know."

"That gives us a place to start. I'll ask a few more questions, and later…" He paused and rested his hand on Lydia's arm for a moment. "Later, you might let me see some of your work."

Lydia laughed. "Is that the equivalent of showing you my etchings sometime?"

"I fell right into that one, but why not?"

"We'll see. Seriously, I have only sketches at the cabin, but I can give you my website. Remind me to give you my card when we get back to the car."

"Good. But I was thinking of something more personal than the Internet. If you have a gallery, we could visit it."

"You'd have to travel some, but yes I have a gallery."

"Excellent."

"By the way, I'm not shy about your seeing my work, but talking about it is a little uncomfortable. It's hard to know how much I should say."

"That seems reasonable, considering you hardly know me."

"It's not that so much. It's more about the way I'm feeling about my art lately."

"You mentioned something about that the other day—that you came here to try to get a fresh start?"

"I don't know if I'm trying to find something here, but it seems like a better place to discover what's blocking me. I've always had lots of ideas, but now I'm second-guessing myself."

"I know that must be difficult for you."

"More than I like to admit, if I'm honest, but I'm sure I'll get things worked out eventually."

She was pleased that John didn't press her for more information and didn't try to offer a solution, the way so many people assumed they could. She could easily imagine a lengthy lecture from one of her colleagues if she dared to confide in them. Even Charles could be unusually wordy at times.

They walked on for another twenty minutes before taking another break.

"Time to take away a layer," she said, tying her jacket around her waist.

John stopped and took an orange from his backpack. After peeling it, he offered a section to her.

"Just what I need. Thank you, John. I brought apples and trail mix for us."

"And I have some energy bars, so we're well-stocked."

They sat beside each other on a log and watched a chipmunk scamper back and forth along the trail in front of them.

"Such energy! I'd like to borrow some of it. I wondered if I would be too slow for you. Are you slowing your pace for me, Lydia?"

"No, but it's not a race, is it? And anyway, I'm not one to rush on a hike like this. I want to see as much as I can and not have to concentrate too much on the time."

"Perfect."

"It's my turn to ask you about your work. You said you're building a house, so I'm guessing you may be a contractor, or maybe that's just an expression?"

"Yes, a contractor. I thought I'd be an architect, but before I'd had many courses, I knew I wanted to be more involved with the actual building of structures. I dropped out of school for a while and worked in construction with my uncle. The school of hard knocks, as my uncle liked to say."

"What school did you go to?"

"Carnegie Mellon."

"Impressive. And you went back?"

"Yes, but this time I took engineering courses and found it was a good foundation for working with both architecture and construction."

"So you saw the connection between the two fields—between the functional and the artistic aspects of your work."

John leaned closer to Lydia until their shoulders were touching. It made Lydia aware of his gentleness and his sexuality. A feeling of warmth and excitement spread through her.

"But you're a long way from Pittsburgh now."

"I've done my share of wandering. And you? Have you been here all of your, let me guess, forty-five years?"

Lydia laughed. "You'll need to add a few."

"You are very attractive, Lydia, and young looking, but that's not really important, is it? We're at the place in our lives when we can see beyond appearances."

John paused, and then took Lydia's hand in both of his and held it firmly and protectively.

"I believe that seeing beyond the surface is one of the most difficult challenges of life. My late wife was somewhat plain physically but possessed a soul more beautiful than I know how to describe. She knew that physical appearances are only a small part of who we are, and she taught me to see that."

"She sounds like a saint."

John laughed. "She would laugh if she could hear you, and she'd tell you she was no saint. She had her faults and temptations like we all do."

"I think that must have been a part of her saintliness."

"What do you mean?"

"People who take themselves too seriously and find fault continually but are unable or unwilling to help themselves or others, don't fit my idea of saintliness. It sounds as if your wife might agree."

"My, such a serious tone we've taken. Let's move on, and I promise we'll have as many serious discussions as you want, but first we need to get around this mountain."

"I don't think there is anything wrong with being serious."

"Not at all."

Silence. Then, they began to speak at the same time. Lydia gestured for John to go first.

"I'm sorry. I didn't mean to be critical."

"It's just me. I'm a little edgy lately. And to be honest, I am a serious person, so I suppose I was afraid you were judging me."

"Ah now, would I do that? Anyway, you've earned A+ marks, Professor."

She laughed and John took her backpack from her and placed it beside his near a boulder. "Let's rest for a minute more, and then we'd better push on so we're back before dark."

"Right. I don't think I'd want to be here at night. Are you good at fending off wild animals?"

"I'd love to take care of you, but I'd probably get an award for running the fastest first."

"I can at least give you bonus points for your honesty then."

A Surprise Visit

Lydia thought about John on her way home. She wanted romance, but she wanted more than a fling. John spoke so lovingly of his wife even though she had died several years ago. It made her wonder if he could be open to romance—whether it would be possible for her to compete with such a perfect ghost.

She glanced at the clock on the dash as she came close to Jan and Bryce's road. It wasn't too late to stop by. Her excuse could be that she was interested in the remodeling she'd heard so much about. Her main purpose, though, was to discover more about them and to ask about the slip of paper in the box. Perhaps she would be able to mask her curiosity a little better with a daytime visit, which would make more sense for a tour of the house and grounds.

As Lydia rounded the last curve on the final stretch toward the cabin, she saw a figure dash across the road. She wasn't sure, but she thought it could be Jan. When she came to the spot, she slowed her car and tried to look into the woods, but she saw only the usual thick forest.

After parking the car and picking up her backpack from the trunk, she looked back to the spot where she had seen the figure. Waiting and listening carefully, she checked for movements, knowing nearly every sound would be audible, but there was nothing.

"Hello? Anyone there? Jan, is that you?"

No answer.

When she reached the porch, she dropped the backpack on one of the rockers and stood at the railing, looking again into the woods, listening again for signs and sounds of movement. Nothing.

She moved quickly inside, telling herself to be calm. She had the cabin owner's phone number, but what would she tell him? *Don't be ridiculous. Calm down.*

A hot shower would relax her, she decided, but remembering the shower scene from *Pyscho* almost changed her mind. Then, she heard crunching on the driveway. Maybe her visitor was returning.

She waited on the porch. Soon Jan came into view.

"Jan, good to see you. Come inside. It's getting chilly out here."

"Happens fast after the sun sets."

"I thought I saw you a little while ago when I was coming up the drive. Was that you?"

"No."

"Who do you suppose it was?"

"I don't know. Are you sure it wasn't an animal? Lots of deer this time of year."

Lydia wondered if Jan was lying, or maybe it was a deer. She motioned to a chair for Jan and put water on for tea.

"I've been enjoying the box you brought me. And I don't know if you know, but there was a square of paper in it."

Lydia opened the box and handed the slip of paper to Jan. She watched Jan unfold it.

"What is it?" Jan asked. "Looks like numbers and letters, but I can't be sure what they are."

"So you didn't know it was in there?"

"No. It must belong to Bryce. I can give it to him, unless you want to," Jan offered.

"I've been thinking about that. In fact, I was even thinking of coming down to your house tomorrow to visit with you so I could find out if the paper was something important."

Lydia reached for the slip of paper and put it back where she had found it.

"That would be great."

"Really? I was a little hesitant, not sure you wanted visitors, but then I thought that since you had come here to see me, it might be okay."

"Definitely. I'll show you the house and more of my work. I mean, if you want to see it."

"I'd love to."

Lydia poured the boiling water into the mugs and placed a tea bag in each. She handed a mug to Jan. "There's something I've been wondering." Lydia wasn't sure, but she thought she saw a shadow cross Jan's face. Was she afraid? "I wondered why neither of you went to college."

"You're not the only person who wonders. I thought about it a lot, and at first I really wanted to go, but Bryce was still in high school, and I hated to leave him behind. And he really didn't want me to leave him."

"But you both could have gone. In fact, it's not too late."

Lydia thought Jan showed a positive response for a moment, but then the brightness in her face dropped away.

"I'd better go. Bryce will be wondering where I am."

"He'll come looking for you again?"

"Probably."

"Does that disturb you?"

Lydia saw Jan grip her hands tightly together before she spoke.

"Sometimes. It's just that he doesn't think . . ." Jan stopped suddenly and stood up. "I really need to go now."

"But you didn't tell me why you came. Is there something I can do for you?"

"No."

Jan moved toward the door, but turned just before opening it. "Miss Lydia, I wanted to tell you something, but I can't now. I really have to go."

"That's all right, Jan. Another time, perhaps?"

"Yeah, perhaps."

Lydia stood on the porch watching after her. The beam of Jan's flashlight flickered through the heavy growth for a few seconds. And Lydia noticed there was scarcely a sound to be heard. Jan was that light on her feet.

Back inside, Lydia sank into the couch. What could be troubling this young woman so much? And who had been in the woods earlier? Could it have been Bryce?

Charles

Charles pulled his BMW into the parking lot beside Sprawls Hall. No trouble parking at this hour of the afternoon. Very few of the faculty opted for a four o'clock class and even fewer chose to teach during the summer.

After so many years of teaching, he could time his arrival perfectly. He relished a margin of time for odds and ends. A cup of coffee. Last-minute review of his lecture notes. He smiled, thinking of Lydia, never late, always early for all of her classes. Since their offices were in the same building, he could count on a brief chat before he started his class.

He hoped she would not become too involved in that little mountain community, particularly with that hiker she'd mentioned. *Not that I'd deprive her of a love life, but I like to have her available.*

Walking across the campus, he thought back to his early years there. So many changes, so much growth. When he was hired, he'd been one of two people in the art department, hardly more than a means of giving students a modicum of art history. If he had succeeded in teaching the difference between Manet and Monet by their senior year, he had done his job. It wasn't a requirement for graduation.

Gradually, under new leadership, the school enlarged, and the art department came into its own, offering both a major and a minor. By the time Lydia was hired, the school claimed a high-caliber faculty and a larger and more sophisticated student body.

He was content with most of the changes. Who would object to better facilities, better salaries, and best of all, sabbaticals with pay, assuming you could snag one? He needed this break. He didn't want to end up a snarling, bitter professor—a bore to his students and his colleagues. Travel and study had always brought renewal for him. A few more good articles and maybe even a book before he hung up his academic robes would be satisfying.

Inside his office, he took a minute to pull up his e-mail and to check his phone messages.

Ah, a message from Simpson, asking for an appointment. He would have another chance to put his sabbatical plans to Simpson in a favorable light.

A knock at his office door reminded him that it was almost time for his art history class.

"Come in."

A tall, severe-looking young man stood in the doorway. "Do you have a minute, Dr. Morris?"

"A brief one. I'm due for class." Charles extended his hand and said, "Pardon me, but I don't seem to know you."

"Bruce Hanson. I just transferred here from Grange College, so you wouldn't know me."

"Right. Mind if we talk while we walk down the hall to my class?"

"Great. I'm looking for an internship and wondered if you could help me. Something in research?"

Charles wondered if the young man was always so intense, but it could be eagerness to achieve his purpose. Not a bad thing in itself. It would be good to work with a serious student.

"Perhaps." He decided not to tell the student he would be away on sabbatical. No sense tempting fate. "If you make an appointment, we can discuss it. You'll find my office hours and phone number posted on my office door. See if something fits your schedule. If not, just give me a call and we'll work out a time."

Charles took an interest in students and enjoyed helping them. The college expected it, and he had never found it a burden. In his early years on campus, he had enjoyed a small following, but now, close to retirement, fewer students stopped by just to chat. His knowledge of pop culture was minimal, other than in the field of art. And even there, he was not as interested as in the earlier periods. He told himself it provided more hours for his own interests if he didn't have students demanding extra attention. Nevertheless, it made the idea of a sabbatical even more attractive.

After his class, Charles hurried back to his office to contact his department chair. He wanted to make his appointment as soon as possible, but Simpson was out of the office. What was wrong with writing a friendly or even a formal note requesting a visit or an appointment? He could count on one hand the number of handwritten notes he'd received in the last few years.

He would have to try again tomorrow. He stuffed a file of course materials and the new issue of *Art in America* into his briefcase, turned off the lights, and locked the door. On the appointment sheet attached to the door, he saw the name of the young man who wanted an internship. He'd requested an afternoon appointment. Would Lydia know this student? She seemed to know all the recent transfer students. Couldn't hurt to call her.

At home, he put a cup of water in the microwave and went to his bedroom for his slippers. A bunion on his left foot demanded relief.

Lydia wasn't answering. Where could she be? Probably a dinner date with that hiker.

He watched *NewsHour* on ETV, made himself a ham and cheese sandwich, and took a beer from the refrigerator before sinking into his favorite reading chair. He turned through a recent issue of *Architect* magazine. An article forecasting new communities designed for the aging population caught his eye.

A young German architect teaching at Penn declared he's old at thirty-nine. *My God, what can he be thinking?* Witnessed his granny's death and decided he has to make a difference for the elderly, a new way to help the mass of boomers survive their extended years. Aided by life-extending procedures up the wazoo, they will have to lead the way for the next generations, he advises.

Just as he was slipping into a nap, his phone rang.

"I'm sorry, Charles. Were you sleeping?"

"Don't worry yourself, dear girl. In fact, I tried to ring you earlier."

"I saw that. Is everything okay?"

"Fine, fine. Reading some young chap's plans for my fellow boomers. Wants to put us up in communities with all the amenities—ever-ready transport, deli-bars, spas, and therapy clinics. Who in their right mind would want to be isolated with all of those old codgers. Not I, for one."

Lydia chuckled. "You do need that sabbatical."

"Indeed I do. However, I need a backup plan in case it doesn't come through. Do you know Bruce Hanson? He says he's a recent transfer student."

"Name sounds familiar. What does he look like?"

"Tall, clean-cut, and very intense. Think Edgar Allen Poe, and you'll have a good picture of him. Wants to do an internship with me. Offered to help with research."

"That's a little unusual. Most of our students these days want something less bookish. They're mostly signed up for the studies abroad or the environmental exploration program if not the ever-popular service program. Save the hungry, see the world, and put it all on the Internet."

Charles laughed. "Aptly put, my dear. Maybe this young man is different.

It could be a breath of fresh air to have a resourceful student working with me."

"When I get back to campus, I'll see what I can find out for you, Charles, but if you're in a hurry, I'll try to track him down via my computer."

"That's my girl, let me know right away, please. By the way, where were you?"

"Why do you ask?"

"So. You were out with your hiker, I gather."

"Stop gathering, Charles."

"You don't mind if I play papa, do you?"

"Don't you mean Big Brother?"

"Depends on your interpretation of the term, doesn't it?"

"It was a very pleasant, but tiring hike, and I'm quite ready for a good sleep, so I'm signing off now."

"Wait. I didn't mean to upset you, Lydia."

"You didn't. I'm just tired. I'll be in touch."

Charles decided the hike must have been less than satisfactory or Lydia would have been in a better frame of mind, not that he minded.

He poured a glass of wine and sank into his couch.

Research. That was a possibility. He'd been delaying the expansion of an article on restoring paintings. He wanted to prove that the older techniques used in restoration were just as good as modern ones, if not better. He'd just read an article that declared cleaning with bread was a viable technique. He imagined the crumb problem and decided he could argue against that procedure with certainty.

Extra research could easily yield a book. He could even begin some of the research himself while on sabbatical. It would be a good combination with his current plan for travel and study in Italy. He smiled—the Italians loved their good bread, and so did he.

BLOCKED

Access to those ancient archives and libraries would be a Godsend and certainly never boring. And perhaps this young man would prove to be helpful, sabbatical or no sabbatical.

Jan

Jan sat against a stack of soft pillows on her bed, struggling with lines of a poem she wanted to finish. She'd begun keeping a journal and writing poems as therapy soon after the accident. Five fat journals sat on her bookshelf near her bed, one for each year since the tragedy.

Staring at the bank of windows that looked into the woods, she remembered how her mother had loved the house and the view. Sometimes they sat there together, her mother in the rocker near the window and she on her bed, talking and talking. Her pretty mother who told her stories about growing up on a farm, going away to college, becoming a teacher, marrying and wanting a baby so much. She told all about trying and trying, and finally adopting two beautiful children, first Jan and later Bryce, to make their little family complete.

Her mother's love she held close to herself, then and now.

She put her pen down and let her thoughts turn toward Miss Lydia. She should have stayed to talk yesterday, but Bryce would have come looking for her. But so what? It was time to do what she wanted. *And how many times have you told yourself that?*

What about college? Could she go, or was it too late, too difficult? Her high school guidance counselor had wanted her to go to college. She'd said that with such good grades and high SAT scores, she could get into any school she wanted. But in the beginning, she had been in no shape to leave her familiar surroundings. She couldn't leave Bryce who was still in high school, and by the time he had graduated, she was in this rut of doing what felt comfortable.

She glanced at her watch and saw that it was time to make some dinner. Bryce would be coming in from the studio soon. She remembered when she had helped Bryce convert the storage room at the back of the garage to the studio. It had taken several weeks, but it had been worth every bit of effort. Sometimes they worked there in silence or with the radio set on the classical music station or on bluegrass, Bryce's favorite. A peaceful haven, especially for Bryce. Without his time in the studio, she thought he might have been in real trouble. It gave him something to focus on.

In the spacious kitchen she stood at the counter watching a squirrel attempting to climb into the large circular birdfeeder hanging from the loblolly pine tree just a few feet from the house. Crafty little bugger was hanging from the top trying to reach under the overhanging cover to grab the seeds. *If I had half as much determination as you, I'd be outta here. Away from this mess.*

From the refrigerator she took sandwich meat and cheese and pickles. She didn't feel like cooking that night. She sliced thick slices of the multigrain bread and covered them with spicy mustard, layered in the meat and cheese, and cut the sandwiches into halves.

Bryce entered the back door and called to her. "Dinner time?"

"Almost ready," she replied.

She poured glasses of sweet tea, put everything on a tray, and carried it to the wraparound porch where they often had their meals during good weather.

"What were you working on today?"

"That box shaped like a heart, the one you told me about. Remember?"

"Right. I thought you said it was silly."

"Changed my mind."

She looked at his half smile, something she had come to hope for. It usually meant he was coming out of one of his dark periods. It might be safe to tell him her plans.

"So you've found a good piece of wood for it?"

"A perfect piece."

"Will it be a puzzle box?"

"Maybe. If it goes well, it could be beautiful as a puzzle."

"It could have a double meaning for someone who wanted to give it as a gift."

"How do you mean?"

"Oh, you know. I can see a man giving it to a woman he loved and saying something like, 'Let this box be a symbol of our love. Two hearts entwined forever.'"

"Ah, playing with words. That's you. Always clever with words."

"And you, too, Bryce. Even when you were just a little boy, you loved words. Mother always said she thought you would be a poet."

"But you're the one who writes poems. Notebooks full of them."

Jan smiled. She loved her brother when he was like this, at ease with her and with himself. *Should I take the risk? A pity, if I spoil it.*

"I thought I'd go visit Miss Lydia after we eat."

Silence.

"You'll be working in the studio for a while after dinner? Right?"

No half smile now.

"Damn it, Jan, why are you messing around over there? You'll get everything upset again."

Jan shivered.

"You've got to learn to trust me, Bryce. Besides, there's something you should know. The box you gave Miss Lydia had a little piece of paper in it—something you must have left in there."

She saw the look of panic come into his eyes.

"I can get it back for you if you want me to."

Bryce shot up from the table, accidently overturning his glass of tea; the fluid ran across the table and onto the floor. "Jesus. Now look what you made me do. Just stay at home where you belong, and everything will work." He rushed out the side door of the screened porch and ran toward the studio. She heard the door slam.

Tears of anger and frustration spilled from her eyes. For so long she had lived with Bryce's temper and his sudden flare-ups. He wouldn't see a doctor. There was no way to get help. But maybe Miss Lydia?

Without even cleaning up the tea that she knew would be a bigger problem later, she rushed to her bedroom to get her backpack and slipped out the door. She was practiced at slipping away and through the woods without a sound.

In the woods, calmness washed over her. These woods—this special place—always had that effect on her. If the studio was a haven for Bryce, the forest was hers.

She felt even more relief when she saw Miss Lydia sitting on her porch. She had half expected her to be there waiting for her. Now she reasoned that this meeting was meant to be.

"Wonderful. You're just in time for dinner, Jan."

"Actually, I've eaten, but I'll keep you company."

"Have some tea at least?"

"Okay."

They sipped their tea and chatted about the good weather and the birds. Jan could see that Lydia wanted her to feel comfortable. She wasn't rushing into personal questions even though she could have after yesterday's exchange. A patient, kind person. *But where do I begin?*

"Miss Lydia, I really need someone to talk to, and I hope that's okay."

"Of course it is."

Jan felt herself relax. She began with the years before the accident. How they were as happy as any family might hope to be. Oh there were arguments and difficulties, but what family didn't have those times? She talked about how close her parents had been, how she felt loved, and Bryce, too. He'd been a happy little boy, always creative and very affectionate. Things had begun to change for him in middle school. Bryce hadn't been able to fit into the rough and tumble world of boys who played sports. He'd always liked quiet activities and was an excellent student.

"I think that's when my parents decided we should move here where the community was small, and there might be more acceptances for Bryce."

"How did you feel about the move, Jan?"

"I didn't want to leave my friends, but I soon fell in love with the woods and the house, especially after we made all the improvements. I want you to see it. My room is really, really nice because of all of the windows that look into the forest."

"Did Bryce like the move too?"

"Oh yes, but he still had more trouble than I did adjusting. I don't know why exactly."

"Sometimes when boys go through puberty they have more problems. Has Bryce had a girlfriend?"

"No, not really. But he might have if it weren't for the accident."

"How old was he when it happened?"

"Just fourteen, a freshman in high school, and I was a senior."

"Such a vulnerable time for both of you. I'm so sorry."

"It might have been worse for me if I hadn't felt it was my responsibility to take care of us. It has certainly made me grow up fast, but now . . . now I want something more for myself, and when you mentioned college, it made me think again about going."

"Oh my dear, I think that would be wonderful for you. I've been thinking about East Valley College where I teach. I see no reason why you wouldn't be happy there, and it's not that far away."

"That's what worries me—being away." Jan paused as she tried to hold back tears. "Bryce? What about him?"

"Do you think Bryce needs some kind of help?"

"Oh yes, definitely." She paused again, waiting to collect herself. "He has such moods, and he's so unpredictable. I've tried everything I know to do, but I can't help. Not enough, anyway."

"And you shouldn't have to, Jan. It's time for both of you to have your own lives. I was wondering about that slip of paper in the box. Did you find out if it was something important?"

"Bryce looked terrible. Kind of wild and full of fear when I mentioned it, and then he stormed out to the studio."

"Let me give it to you so you can return it to him. Let's not push for answers right now."

Lydia went inside to the coffee table and retrieved the piece of paper from the box.

"Okay. I think I'd better leave now, Miss Lydia. Maybe we can talk again soon? You won't be here forever, and I want to get things going."

"I'll be here, but you're right to want to get started on your plans. Maybe we can arrange for you to come to the campus for a visit."

"I would love that, but what about Bryce?"

"We'll invite him to come too."

"I don't think he'll come."

"Perhaps not, but we'll include him and let him decide."

"Should I tell him?"

"You will have to decide that. From what you've told me, I think Bryce may be afraid that you are going to leave him, and he doesn't know how he would handle being left here. In some ways, he may never have had a chance to recover properly from your parents' death. Much can be accomplished with a good counselor, but the person has to be willing to take it on. He may not be able to do that as long as you're here for him to lean on."

"I've read a zillion articles and some books trying to figure out what to do, but every time I tried to get Bryce to go with me to a doctor, he freaked out."

"It can be a very frightening idea in the beginning. Come for lunch tomorrow?"

"If I can get away."

John

After John left Lydia at her car, he drove straight home, a twenty-minute drive to the other side of the mountain. He thought about Lydia, confident and yet sensitive, two qualities he liked in a woman. Kind of serious, although that was a good line about seeing her etchings. An obvious love for nature, which he was glad they shared, and he liked the way she showed an interest in his past and his work.

He wondered if he'd talked too much about Nancy. *I suppose I'll have to put a cap on that if I'm to win Lydia's favor.* He knew most women wanted a man who would concentrate on them exclusively, at least while in their presence. But it had been so natural to talk about Nancy. He was so lonely most of the time, especially when he wasn't working. Marriage? He wasn't ready for that, but it would be good to be with a woman again.

He thought things had gone well on the hike, and if that continued, he would definitely put some effort into keeping her interested. Best to take it slow. It wouldn't do to get tangled in something messy. He'd always heard that artists were temperamental and difficult, the ego factor. He wondered if he was prepared for that, not after Nancy, always so sweet and easy-going. He reminded himself again that continuing to make comparisons wasn't good.

As soon as he got home and finished his quick pick-up meal of hamburger and salad, he went to his office to look over his plans for tomorrow's work. He expected to have the rest of the interior details of the house completed by winter. If he couldn't stick to his schedule, he'd have to hire some help, but he really wanted to do it all himself, every last nail, all of the tiny finishing details. He'd poured his heart into this house, and he didn't want any sloppy workmanship—not his and certainly not anyone else's.

For his construction company, he was a demanding but fair foreman; he expected his workers to give their best. Perfection he'd seen in his father's and grandfather's examples had stayed with him and had been further enhanced by his training. Their love in creating and their sense of pride gave him the impetus to take every part of every job seriously. He worked at instilling the same attitude in his workers, and if he failed in getting a high quality performance from them, he let them go. It was important to him that his construction company to be known as both honorable and reliable.

He looked at the floor plan, wondering what Lydia would think of it. Probably not enough room devoted to the kitchen; most women wanted an expansive kitchen even if they didn't cook a great deal. Nancy had been an excellent cook and had loved the kitchen they'd planned together, but he preferred a simple Pullman style workspace. Streamlined. Everything easy to reach.

He loved this house, mostly because of its commanding view, looking across the valley to the next mountain. The house sat on an acre of land he'd partially cleared, leaving the forest behind the house but taking enough away to provide a view on two sides. The steep winding road leading to the house could prove to be a problem in the heart of winter if it weren't for four-wheel drive, a small detail for him, but he realized it could be a negative for anyone not used to driving in the mountains, a point he and Nancy had considered briefly when they purchased the property.

Tall windows across the front of the house gave him the feeling of owning the distant mountains. The deck that wrapped around the front and south sides of the house gave ample space for outside relaxation and provided the best two possible views on the site.

Funny how the plans for the house had evolved. Initially, he and Nancy planned it for a vacation home that they could use and then sell. But when Nancy died, everything changed. For a while, he had shelved the plans, not able to think about them, wanting to escape all the pain. Eventually, he decided to build only an efficient cabin, but then he realized he'd like to have enough space for guests. And for resale value, it made sense to make it large enough for a family, not that he planned to sell it, not for a long time, if ever. Still, it was only practical to think of all the possibilities.

He leaned back in his office chair and reached for the phone, but first he had to give his cat some attention. His Maine Coon cat was totally unpredictable except for a few set routines. Scrap demanded to have "desk time" at least once a day, usually in the evening, probably because that's where his master ended up most evenings, planning work for the next day. He obediently stroked the cat's long, thick fur and promised to give him a real brushing in a few minutes.

"Okay, Scrap, that's enough for now. I've got to make a date with an important lady." The cat seemed agreeable as he leapt off the desk and settled into one of his soft cushions John had placed near the desk.

"Lydia, just checking to see if you made it home okay."

"How thoughtful. Yes, I'm fine. Pleasantly tired. And you?"

"A fine day, and pleasantly tired is a good description for me too."

Silence.

"I'm just sitting here in my office looking at the plans, and it occurred to me that I'd like to show you my house, even though it's not finished. I still have dry-walling to do in the upper bedrooms, but it's basically livable. Electricity and plumbing are in and working. No landscaping, but naturally there won't be much. I prefer having the natural forest left in back of the house, and the front looks off toward the mountains."

"A view of the mountains, always marvelous."

"Nancy and I chose the site for its view. I've done a lot of the work myself, so it's been rather slow, but I think I can finish by winter. That's my goal, anyway."

Another silence.

John told himself he had to stop mentioning Nancy.

"Anyway, could I pick you up tomorrow afternoon?"

"I'd like that, but unfortunately I've already made plans. The young woman who lives on the next property is coming to talk with me about college. She may enroll at Spring Valley."

"Ah, so perhaps another time?"

"Yes, certainly. A friend of mine may be coming for a visit in a while, but after that, would be fine."

"Good. We'll make it happen. I'll call you."

John admonished himself for not making a date with Lydia after their hike, but perhaps it was for the best. He needed to keep working. He'd have more to show her if he got busy, maybe hired some help. It would be an extra incentive to keep a full schedule. Wanting to enjoy the spring and summer weather hiking and fishing, he'd become slack, and when his brother asked him to give him a hand with his young son, he'd been relieved to have the distraction.

His thoughts turned toward Josh. Such a good kid. He hoped for his sake that he wouldn't be hurt too much by the divorce. Maybe he would like to come for the weekend for another hike or some fishing. Or some kayaking. The more he pondered the idea, the more it appealed.

He wondered if Lydia liked water sports, probably, since she was obviously a devotee to nature. That was one thing Nancy had never enjoyed. She'd sent him off for some meditation time, as she liked to call it, while she explored new recipes and laid plans for a dinner party. Not a bad plan, having some time apart. He wondered if his brother could have saved his marriage if he'd had the wisdom to follow a similar pattern. But who could solve someone else's problems? Pure folly to even think such a thing.

"What do you think, Scrap? Want me to invite Josh for a visit? You two bonded when Josh was here last time."

John took a brush from the bottom drawer of his desk and bent to give Scrap his nightly brushing. The cat turned to lick his master's hand.

More Time with Jan

Lydia wondered, as she dawdled over her lunch, if she should have suggested another time to see John's house. It would be interesting to see the location and his design ideas, but honestly she was more interested in seeing John. Would he call again, or was he just being polite? Better to let it drop. She doubted he was interested in more than casual friendship. And that was okay, she conceded.

She leaned over the deck, watching for any action in the woods. A tiny chipmunk scurried around a tree trunk and under the deck, not the first time she'd seen him. "Unless that's your brother or sister?" She smiled.

"Caught you talking to the animals, Miss Lydia."

Lydia laughed. "Jan, your stealth amazes me. How do you do it? Would it be offensive if I suggested that you may have Indian blood? Oops, I mean Native American blood."

Lydia noticed Jan's look of confusion. "Oh you know, we have to be politically correct these days."

"Right." Jan hesitated before going on. "You do know that I'm adopted? So, who knows? I may have Indian blood. But then maybe not, with this blonde hair."

"Yes, I know about the adoption, but I was only thinking that you are especially quiet in your approach, not that it's a problem."

"I guess I've practiced enough to be a pro at it. I remember how my mom teased me about slipping up on her. She said I was in training to become a spy."

"It sounds like you had a good relationship with your mother. When I think about how you had to go from being a carefree young girl to being totally responsible for you and Bryce, it amazes me."

Jan looked down at her lap, and Lydia suspected tears were being held in check.

They were silent for a time as the two rockers struck up a gentle rhythm and streaks of sunlight broke through the treetops and across the deck, creating scattered patterns on their faces and arms.

Jan cleared her throat and said, "I'm interested in college, but I'd like to talk about something else first."

Lydia was pleased that Jan seemed to be taking the lead. "Of course."

"It's more about Bryce. Bet that doesn't surprise you."

Lydia heard the change in Jan's voice, an edge of something. Sadness? Or perhaps anger?

"Is it about the slip of paper?"

"Sort of. He didn't want to tell me what it was, but he was glad to get it back, so I know it's important. Maybe when he's in a good mood, I can ask him about it."

"I wouldn't push it, but you'll probably know if there's a right time."

They were silent for a few moments.

"Do you think you could talk with Bryce? Maybe he'd listen to you."

Lydia was surprised and couldn't think of how she should answer.

"I doubt very much that Bryce would want to talk with me, Jan."

"But he might. He respects you because you're an artist. You could show him your work."

"I don't have any work here. Just some sketches."

"That would be okay, wouldn't it?"

"I could show him pictures of my work on my computer."

"Great. I was sure you would help."

"Actually, I'm still very concerned about the way he treats you. You told me yesterday some things about his behavior, how moody he is at times. I wondered if he's been abusive to you." Lydia paused. "Has he?"

"Abusive? No, but if only he had a girlfriend, I think that would solve lots of stuff for him."

"I didn't necessarily mean sexual abuse. I meant physical or emotional abuse."

Lydia saw the puzzled look in Jan's eyes. She waited.

"If you're asking if he's ever hit me, I can tell he wants to sometimes, and if our parents hadn't been terribly strict about that, he might do it, but I don't think he'd ever mean to hurt me. He gets so angry, you know? But then he goes to the studio and works out of it."

"So he doesn't hit you. I'm glad. But emotional abuse?"

Jan stopped her rocker and turned to look at Lydia.

"Emotional abuse can come in several different ways. It can be withholding love or praise or even refusing to speak. It might be some form of belittling, making you feel as if you were the cause of his problems."

"Yeah, maybe. I just think it's frustration that he has to let out, and I'm the only one around. Besides, I'm older and I kind of expect it and ought to be able to take it."

Lydia sat quietly, wondering if she should go on. Was it right to talk about things she wasn't really qualified to discuss? She remembered when she first began teaching at Spring Valley, a situation had come up that caused Charles to warn her about getting too close to the students. He'd said, "Remember, we aren't counselors. We have people on campus trained to do this, so send the student to the Counseling Center." At first, she thought he was being too severe, but later she came to understand. Without realizing it, a teacher could easily put herself in a compromising position, which could turn ugly if the student suddenly decided to use or misuse information against the teacher. Both the student and the teacher could be hurt. But Jan needed someone to listen, didn't she? Surely, there was no harm if she just listened.

Lydia said, "I think it is not a good idea to be the object of any kind of abuse, but it's not easy to know what to do."

Jan lowered her head, and her rocker slowed and then stopped.

Lydia feared Jan had misunderstood.

"So you mean that if I let Bryce treat me bad, I'm wrong? It's my fault?"

"I suppose it sounds like that, but I'm not placing blame, and honestly I don't think anyone could handle things any better than you have, Jan."

Jan reached into her pocket for a tissue, and Lydia knew this was not what she had wanted. She reached to pat Jan's shoulder.

"I'm sorry. I didn't mean to hurt you."

"It's okay. I just don't know what to do."

"You mentioned that your high school guidance counselor had wanted you to go to college. Is the counselor still at your high school?"

"Mrs. Stafford? Yeah, I'm pretty sure. I still see her at the Market sometimes."

"I think she would be a good person to talk with you about all of this and about going to college. She knows that you were left to take care of Bryce after your parents' accident, so she will understand your situation when you tell her about it. And she can help you prepare the application for college, get your transcripts, and write a letter of reference for you."

Suddenly, light came into Jan's face.

During the rest of the visit, Lydia spent some time answering Jan's questions about Spring Valley College and describing some of the college's programs.

Jan left, saying that she would let her know what happened with Mrs.

Stafford.

By that time, Lydia was feeling cheered but suddenly in need of a nap. She lay on the bed with a soft throw across her legs, and was asleep almost immediately.

☙

Lydia woke suddenly from her dream. Sweat rolled from her body, and the throw was twisted around her. As she stood, she felt slightly dizzy. Reaching for the doorway, she stood for a moment to steady herself before moving into the bathroom. When she glanced in the mirror above the sink, she saw the remnants of shock on her face.

She didn't want to remember the dream, but she had no choice.

She had been walking through the woods on her way to visit Jan. Everything seemed fine at first. She remembered how pleasant it was; the scent of pine, a light breeze creating in the treetops, and the chorus of bird songs. Then she heard crunching sounds from behind her, but when she turned to see what it might be, nothing was there. She walked on, but only moments later, she heard the crunching again, so she began to walk faster and faster, and then to run. Someone or something was chasing her, and she had to get away.

That's when she woke.

It had been a long time since she'd had a frightening dream, possibly not since childhood. She couldn't think of a time when she had been gripped by such intense fear.

In the kitchen, she poured a glass of water and returned to the couch to try to collect herself, but she remained anxious. Not being a true believer in dream analysis, she told herself to forget the dream, but could it be a warning?

The Storm

That night, Lydia paced around the small cottage, rubbing her forehead, pausing to look outside at the approaching storm. Normally, she enjoyed a sudden storm with its dramatic changes: the streaks of lightning, followed by crashing, rolling thunder, gusts of wind, and sheets of driving rain. But this time, her inner turmoil prevented any satisfaction in nature's show. A ball of tangled strings pulled at her, making her feel like a small child overwhelmed by confusion.

She had not been an easily disturbed person, not until her recent discovery that her creative powers were threatened.

She knew that she should put aside the list, should concentrate on one problem at a time, should withdraw from any feelings of *should*. A dim memory came to her mind of a time her friend Charles had remarked, "You are allowing yourself to be dominated by a list of *shoulds*. Until you move away from that list, you'll be incapacitated. Try tackling one of them, and see where it leads you."

There were the Jan and Bryce issues, the John questions, the Charles concerns, and most of all her painting problems. *So where should I begin?*

She poured a glass of wine and carried it to her favorite chair. In the darkness of the storm, the lamplight spread a soft glow around her, which normally would soothe her. Not tonight.

Even though her talk with Jan had gone well, she had misgivings. She believed Jan continued to hide something important. If she were to believe Jan's story, Bryce suffered only from moodiness. Surely bouts of moodiness would not be enough to cause Jan to be fearful. Yet fear was the feeling Jan had emitted again and again.

Had she made a mistake sending Jan to her high school counselor? There was no way of knowing the counselor's skills or effectiveness. *Why did you allow yourself to get involved?* Maybe that was the meaning of her dream, but for now there was nothing to do but wait.

The lights began to flicker, and then a loud crack that sounded as if it were only feet away from the cabin told Lydia that she needed to make some plans. She went to the kitchen to look for candles and matches, knowing the power might be knocked out at any moment. She looked in all of the cabinets and drawers until she found at the back of one of the cupboards a large flashlight. That would have to do. She placed it on the coffee table where she could find it in the dark.

Instructions she'd heard hundreds of times came back to her. Stay away from windows and find cover under a large table or in a closet or the bathroom. There was no large table, and the bathroom had a window, so she ruled those out. She hated the idea of being stuck in the closet, but that was a possibility if things got worse.

Not knowing how long she might be stuck, she took an apple, some nuts, and a carton of juice and some bottled water from the refrigerator and placed them in a shopping bag inside the closet.

The lightning flashed so intensely, it felt as if a huge searchlight were shining on the cabin, and the thunder rolled louder and louder. The wind roared and debris flew past the windows.

A sudden crash, only feet away from the cabin, had to be a tree coming down, but Lydia knew she couldn't check it. She needed to go ahead and take shelter in the closet, as much as she hated the idea.

Rain began to pummel the cabin, and the wind blew so hard it made a high-pitched whistle. She grabbed a pillow from the couch and the flashlight and went inside the closet where she sank down to sit on the cushion. At least the smell of cedar in the closet was pleasant.

She shivered, imagining what might happen if one of the giant pines fell across the cabin. Her imagination ran wild with different scenarios. What if she were trapped inside this closet with no way to get out for days? How long could she survive? Would anyone come looking for her? Would the road be passable? Would they have equipment to get to her?

Pulling a blanket from the top shelf of the closet, she made a nest for herself and got as comfortable as possible. She would ration her food and liquids, in case she was blocked in there.

"I probably should have brought a book with me." Then she laughed. "Forget that. I should have brought the wine with me. And an opener."

She laughed again. "There you go with that should stuff. Time for you to move on. Okay, but first I have to get through this storm. Charles, when I see you again, I'm going to wring your neck for sending me up here. If I could get a signal on my cell phone, I'd call you right now and let you have it."

Another crash on the other side of the cabin sounded like an even larger tree.

What should she do to keep from having a panic attack? She certainly wasn't going to be able to sleep. She decided to eat an apple very slowly, just one bite, and then wait and wait, and then another bite. Then one nut and one tiny sip of water. And then another nut.

A loud banging sound on the porch must be the rockers being smashed. "Oh, not those lovely rockers."

"Oh my God, what if I have to go to the bathroom? What a revolting thought. I guess I'll just wait and see. Better not drink for now."

The rain and wind raged on and on. Lydia grew more and more tense in her cramped position. She could stand up for a while to relieve her legs, but the closet was quite small. She decided to open the door a crack, but it was too dark to see anything. Perhaps at the next flash of lightning, she could assess things.

She waited and waited.

The wind was subsiding, or at least she thought it was. She'd had the roaring in her head for so long, she wondered if she were capable of determining what she was hearing.

"It's time to get gone, you crazy bastard of a storm. If nothing else, I've got to get to the bathroom." She knew when she gave her account of this storm she would probably not let anyone know she had been carrying on a conversation with the storm half the night, but it had served a good purpose.

Gingerly, she left her nest. Water had blown under the door across the cabin floor. The wind had been that strong. Just as she had expected, the rockers were in a broken heap at one corner of the porch, and a large pine tree lay just feet away across the path that led to her car. She worried that her car might be smashed, but she decided not to go out until daylight.

The wind was subsiding, so she decided to try for a few hours of sleep.

ಔ

She woke to someone calling her name.

She pulled on her jeans and a shirt before going to the door.

Outside, just beyond the pine that lay across the path, George Randolph stood.

"Thank God you're okay, Lydia. Ruth and I have been worried, but we had to wait until morning to check on you. That storm came with a vengeance."

"I'd invite you in for coffee, but there's no power," she said.

"Right. Let's see if we can get you down here, and I'll take you to the house for some breakfast."

"Sounds good. I'll be right with you." She put on her gym shoes and grabbed a jacket. The sun was out and the sky crystal clear with a chill in the air.

"You're going to have to travel to the foot of this pine unless you want to try to climb over it, and I wouldn't advice that. Can you get through by coming around this way?"

Lydia made her way through the patches of debris and loose branches until she was standing beside George.

"That was some storm."

"Sure enough, it was a doozy."

Lydia was glad to climb into the truck, which looked secure enough to manage anything anywhere, and head for coffee. "What was that anyway, a hurricane?"

George laughed. "Believe me, if it was, I wouldn't have been able to get up here. The trees would have been laid out like toothpicks most likely. I was caught in Hugo back in '89 while visiting a friend who had a little place near Charleston. Now that was a hurricane for sure."

"What happened?"

"We decided to wait it out, and it was a very, very long night. That wind was worse than the freight train you always hear about. It just wouldn't let up, and your body is so tense from waiting for something to happen, you're sore from top to bottom the day after."

"I remember that storm, but not because I was in it. We didn't have much more than some high wind in the interior, but I had students whose families were on the coast, and they were so upset. They all wanted to get home as soon as possible to see the damage. In some cases, it was lucky for them that they weren't at home when Hugo hit."

"There was plenty to be thankful for when you heard about how bad some had it. We fired up the grills to cook what was in the freezer because without power, everything was going to spoil. We ended up turning the disaster into a party."

"My students talked about that. They said that the chainsaws were running from early morning until night. They brought back pictures that were amazing. Pine trees chopped off in the middle and live oaks uprooted and lying across the tops of houses and cars, debris everywhere. I told them to draw it and use it in their art. For some, it was a kind of therapy."

"Using it in their art? Now I would never have thought of that. Seems like art should be something beautiful."

"That's the usual thinking, but some artists have capitalized on the ugly. I think of Francis Bacon who showed the grotesque side of images. Lots of death imagery, misshapen figures and faces, and nothing beautiful."

"But who would want to hang that on their walls and be scared every time they looked at it?"

Lydia laughed. "I know what you mean, but another way to think about it is the fact that not everything in life portrays beauty. I have a friend whose husband was so taken by the mummified corpses in a museum in Mexico that he spent months painting nothing but mummies when he came home."

"Just give me a simple mountain scene for my walls, thank you."

"Actually, I could do that for you, George. I'd like to give you one of my drawings. Just a simple rendition of your cabin."

"Say now, that's an awful nice thing to do, but maybe you'd better wait until we get through cleaning up this storm. You might change your mind about how good your time has been."

BLOCKED

Inside George and Ruth's house, drinking their cups of coffee and eating thick slices of Ruth's homemade bread, toasted and buttered, the storm was forgotten.

Ruth said, "I'm glad you came down the mountain this morning, Lydia. We're sorry we couldn't come get you last night. I know that had to be terrible for you."

"I wasn't going to tell anyone, but I had a pretty good time scolding that storm last night."

They continued to talk, and then Ruth gave Lydia the opening she needed.

"I've had a soft spot in my heart for those two young people ever since the accident. It was such a pity that, well, you know, being adopted, there was no family to take them in. I don't imagine any adoption agency would have had a chance of placing a couple of nearly grown teenagers either. And there was the problem with Bryce."

"The problem?" Lydia asked.

"Oh yes, the boy has never been totally right, but the accident just made everything worse."

"Now Ruth, I don't think Lydia wants to get into this."

"Actually, George, I do. I've noticed from the beginning the way Bryce treats his sister, and it is not what I'd call normal. Jan has seemed so fearful when she's come to visit me, as if something would happen if she didn't hurry right back home."

"She's come visiting, has she? Well, I'm glad to hear it," Ruth said.

"Yes, she told me that Bryce has moods and that she's worried about him. I've told her to talk with her high school guidance counselor about that and about going to college. I could help her get off to a good start at Spring Valley where I teach."

Lydia watched for a reaction but noticed only the reluctance for either to speak.

"Jan told me that she'd gotten excellent grades and that her counselor had wanted her to go to college."

Jan watched Ruth working her fingers together nervously.

"If you don't mind my asking, what is Bryce's problem?"

George got up from his chair and stood beside his wife with his hand on her shoulder. "There are some things that need to be left alone."

Ruth looked up at him and then at Lydia. "And there's a time when things need to be said, to be let out in the open, and this may be one of them."

"Please, I assure you I have only the best interests of these young people in mind. If there is information that could be helpful, I hope you will share it."

Ruth looked up at her husband before she spoke. "We only know the rumors." He nodded yes and sat down again.

"I'm against spreading rumors," George said.

"Usually, I am, too," Lydia said, "but I think I need information before I can be of help to these young people."

"How do you think you can help?" George asked.

Lydia paused. "Truthfully, I'm not sure that I can, but I want to, and I sense that you do too."

Ruth cleared her throat. "It all goes back to the reason they moved here from Atlanta. We wouldn't have known about it if we hadn't had friends in Atlanta who lived in the same neighborhood and told us the story.

"Our friends told us all about the trouble Bryce was having in school with fights and not fitting in. It didn't sound so unusual to us since most times kids can have some of that kind of trouble. Some kids are just naturally mean, especially when they find a weak spot.

"Well, it happened that the school children found out that Bryce was adopted, and either they made up a story or they got some facts. It's hard to tell for sure."

Ruth got up to pour fresh coffee.

"Anyway, the story was that Bryce's mother was raped, but she wouldn't have an abortion even though the man was a violent criminal. Our friends remembered the fuss that was made in the papers and on TV about it for weeks and weeks. They thought the mother must have been a little crazy. Well, you know how some of these stories go these days. I swan, I don't know what's coming over the world. It's just awful the terrible things happening everywhere."

George coughed.

"So the Johnsons must have decided that they couldn't live there with all of that gossip and the hardship it was creating for their children, and they moved up here. Said they'd always loved the mountains and were ready to get out of the big city."

"How did they choose Hollyville?" Lydia asked.

George said, "Sam Johnson was in real estate and investments, and that's the kind of thing you can do most anywhere. He was a friendly, likeable guy, and it wasn't long before he and his wife, too, fit in as if they'd been born here.

"Bought that place for next to nothing and turned it into a regular showplace with all the changes and additions. He was doing great. Just a damn shame he had to have that accident coming home that night. Might 'a had a little too much to drink at the dance, I expect."

Ruth reached over to pat her husband's arm. "We all took to them. Vicki was pretty as a picture and got busy in the community organizing fundraisers to add an addition to the library. Some of us said that if she'd run for office, we'd elect her mayor without blinking an eye."

George added, "Yes, and a good mother to those children. Bryce was getting into his art and fitting in without a problem. Smart as anything."

"So you think Bryce is still troubled by the rumors and wants to find his mother, perhaps to discover the truth, especially now that his adoptive mother is gone?" Lydia asked.

"It sure seems like it," Ruth said.

Guidance for Jan

Jan read her lines again and again, looking for the right words to keep the poem going. The seed for the poem had come from her last visit with Miss Lydia. College bound? Could it actually happen, or was it still an idle dream?

> New doors and windows open wide,
> Offering a bright new way
> Yearnings hidden for so long
> Spin and churn on a long, delicate thread
> Lifting ever up and away
>
> Away from anger and frustration
> Away from fear and confusion

Jan remembered how her English teachers had offered encouragement to write, to keep a journal, to work on her fiction and poetry. Her guidance counselor had given her folders about choosing a career, had said she could go to any college of her choice, that she would help her find scholarships.

But Bryce. That was and is the problem. Never mind—today is my day.

BLOCKED

Jan arrived early for the appointment she'd made with Ms. Stafford. In the outer office, she was told to relax and wait a few minutes while Ms. Stafford finished a conference with a student. She picked up the recent issue of the school's newspaper, *The Tiger*, and scanned the articles, looking for familiar names. So soon most of the names are gone. Teachers and coaches retired or moved on to new jobs, new marriages, new locations.

"Jan, Ms. Stafford will see you now."

Jan dropped the newspaper on the table, straightened her shoulders, and gave herself a mental jab: *You can do this.*

"Jan, I'm so glad to see you. I've often seen you from a distance around town, but we haven't had a chance to talk, so this is a wonderful surprise."

Jan smiled and took the seat Ms. Stafford indicated. She saw that Ms. Stafford's dark hair showed patches of grey and her laugh lines were deeper, but she still had that smile and warmth that made her so popular with the students.

"Now bring me up to date. What have you been doing, besides your wonderful crafts that I've seen at the Market?" She turned in her chair and pointed to one of Jan's small shadow boxes resting on the bookcase.

Jan, feeling relaxed, almost as if she were a high school student again, just stopping by for a chat, as she had done so often her senior year, talked freely about her art projects and her writing—all of the things she knew Ms. Stafford would approve of.

"I can see that you're staying busy. It's wonderful that you are continuing to use your talent."

Jan almost failed to notice when Ms. Stafford moved from the easy, everyday kind of talk into the serious topic.

"I've thought about you so often, wondering what happened to your plans for college."

"That's one of the reasons I've come to see you, Ms. Stafford. I want to apply for college."

"Wonderful! Tell me more."

Jan told her about Miss Lydia's proposal that she go to Spring Valley College, that she get some help with the necessary paper work. She didn't mention her problem with Bryce.

"I'll be glad to help you with any of that, Jan. But first, tell me a little about your new friend. Lydia?"

"She's renting the cabin from the Randolphs on the mountain. You know, it's not far from our place in the woods. I've gotten to know her because she's an artist. And an art professor at Spring Valley. She came to the Market to see our artwork. Well, mostly to see Bryce's boxes, I think, but anyway she's really nice."

"Good, good. So you trust her. That's very important."

"Sure. Why not?"

"No particular reason. But sometimes you need to be careful. It's not always easy to know if a person is being honest."

"Being honest? Why wouldn't she be honest?"

"I'm just saying that it's necessary these days to be a little careful, even a bit suspicious."

"She thinks I should go to college so I can have something for myself." Jan turned slightly and looked out the window. Why was Ms. Stafford being suspicious? *She doesn't know Lydia, but I do.*

"You remember, Jan, that *I* wanted you to go to college so you could have something for yourself, but you chose to stay here. Is there some reason you should go to college now? What's brought on this sudden change?"

Jan noticed the change in Ms. Stafford's voice. Something was wrong. She seemed almost angry.

"I need to get away."

"Tell me what's wrong. Something must be troubling you to cause this sudden change."

"I just have to get away. That's all."

"Get away? From what?"

"From Bryce."

Ms. Stafford leaned back in her chair. "Yes, I suspected as much."

Ms. Stafford was quiet, looking down at the papers in front of her, appearing to be suddenly uninterested in Jan.

Jan stood up suddenly. "I came here because I thought you could help me, but I must have made a mistake."

"Don't go, Jan. We need to talk. I'm thinking about the best way to handle your situation."

"You don't need to handle it. I'll do it myself."

Jan moved toward the door. Ms. Stafford moved away from her desk and toward Jan.

"I'm sorry, Jan. I didn't mean to offend you. Please, let's talk some more. Surely, you must know how concerned I am for you and your brother. You must also know that leaving Bryce will bring new problems for you."

Jan turned back toward her counselor, took a tissue from her pocket, and wiped at her tears. "I know, but what can I do? It's such a mess, and I'm so tired."

"Oh my dear, yes, I know. It has been a heavy burden for a long time." Ms. Stafford hugged Jan for a moment before returning to her chair and gesturing to Jan to sit down again.

"Bryce is okay lots of the time, especially when he has his artwork, and as long as I stay there with him and do everything quietly the way he wants me to. He goes crazy if I'm ever gone very long. He came to get me when I visited Miss Lydia, and back at the house he had one of his fits throwing things and shouting awful things."

"He has needed counseling, even before your parents' accident, Jan. The anger and frustration in that young man has been growing. I've worried about it for a long time, but there hasn't been anything I could do."

Jan began to sob. She took another tissue Ms. Stafford handed her and wiped her eyes and nose. "I want to do the right thing."

"It's only right that you should have a chance to find a life for yourself. This may seem like a strange idea, but have you thought about trying to find your parents?"

"Sometimes, but Bryce is the one who needs parents. I can take care of myself, especially if I can have a career. But my artwork and my writing aren't enough, Ms. Stafford. Art is everything to Bryce. Without it, he'd really be completely crazy." Jan faltered on the word *crazy* as if she has had finally revealed her deepest fear.

A look of empathy passed over Ms. Stafford's face, and there was a moment of silence.

"Has Bryce ever indicated that he wants to find his parents?"

"Not exactly, but once I saw on the computer all this search stuff he'd done that looked kinda suspicious to me. Maybe that's what he was doing. And there's something else. Miss Lydia found a little note Bryce left in the box he gave her. When I told him about it, he got really strange and stormed off to the studio."

"Bryce gave Miss Lydia one of his boxes with a note inside it?"

"Yes. She came to the Market and wanted to buy several boxes but couldn't because she didn't have cash. You know how we have to be careful about checks and all, so he wouldn't take her check. Later, he felt bad about it and told me to take the box to her because he knew she really liked his work."

More silence.

Ms. Stafford turned in her chair to pick up Jan's shadow box. She held it and traced its edges with her finger.

"Bryce made it. I just added the scene inside it."

Ms. Stafford sighed deeply and shook her head slightly.

"Sometimes with talent and artistry come great pain and turmoil. I've known for a long time that Bryce was suffering. We saw it when both of you were students here. Occasionally, one of the teachers would talk with me about Bryce, wondering how to help him."

"I think my parents moved here because they wanted to give us another chance. Things were really messed up for him in Atlanta with fights and everything, but here he got into art more, and it was better."

Jan glanced at her watch. "I have to go. Bryce thinks I've gone to the grocery store, and he'll be looking for me."

Ms. Stafford shook her head.

Lost

George took away the rockers to see if they could be repaired and hired a man to cut up the fallen tree and clean up most of the debris around the cabin. Things were back to normal—at least for the cabin.

Lydia sat on the wide porch rail looking up into the trees. The way the sunlight created lacy patterns with the leaves dancing in the wind, catching and then losing the light, fascinated her. It made her think again about her painting with its threads of light, what her student Anne had at first called a prison. She thought about a string of problems she'd conquered in the past with almost no trouble. She'd never had a breakdown, so thought of herself as a resilient, well-adjusted person. Other people were thrown into depression following the death of a parent or the loss of a job, the break-up of a relationship or marriage, a battle with a major illness. She hadn't dealt with all of those issues, but she'd had her fair share.

Her entire family had been dealt a heavy blow when her youngest sister had come home from college thinking she had the flu, but she never returned to college. It wasn't the flu or even a physical illness. It was the beginning of schizophrenia that kept her, and to some extent the entire family, a prisoner for the next twenty-five years while she was in and out of the mental hospital, in one group home after another, and finally caught in the throes of cancer.

Thinking of her sister took Lydia back to Bryce. It certainly seemed from Jan's description of his behavior as if he were struggling with some type of mental illness, at least with depression or perhaps with a bipolar disorder.

Had she been wrong to pass Jan off to her high school counselor?

And what was she to make of the story Ruth Randolph had passed along to her, much against her husband's wishes? Did it matter that Bryce's mother was a girl who'd been raped by a violent criminal? Assuming it was true, how would it help Bryce to learn this information? If anything, it might cause him greater trouble. She decided the Randolphs had good reason to keep quiet.

Lydia worried over what she should do with this new information. Her heart hurt for these two young people, both of them left to find their own way. If only they could have a good counselor to help them. If Bryce came to see her artwork, perhaps she'd have an opportunity to help, to draw him out and to find out what troubles bothered him most.

Lydia let her mind drift. *Here I am trying to solve someone else's problems when I have no idea of how to solve my own. Pathetic.*

"Enough! I'm going for a walk."

She exchanged her sandals for her hiking boots, filled her water bottle, and set off in the direction she'd seen Jan take after one of her visits. It shouldn't be too difficult to find the Johnson place.

At first, the terrain was level and easy, despite the effects of the recent storm, but soon she found she was working hard to find secure footing. The angle of the slope increased to the extent that she had to hang on to small trees to prevent sliding down the mountainside. "How does Jan do this? Maybe I should have taken the road."

After twenty minutes, she was overheated and needing water, so she sat on a boulder to recover, surprised that she was finding this hike to be so difficult.

Lydia laughed at herself. "Maybe I'm going to live out my problems physically from now on, but let's hope I'm not like King Sisyphus rolling the stone up the hill again and again."

Fortunately, the sun gave her a sense of direction, but had she made the false assumption, that Jan and Bryce's house was a straight shot to the north of her cabin? Surely, she would have come to the house by now.

"Don't panic. You can do this."

But fifteen minutes later, she still saw no sign of anything but dense forest.

"Great. Now I'm lost. If I'm traveling in a circle, does that mean I'll end back at the cabin? If not, I'll come to the road."

She labored on, taking water breaks, looking carefully for signs of a trail. If Jan walked these woods often, she must have a trail that she followed.

It was past noon. She'd been wandering around for over an hour. She sat down to eat an apple and to rest. She had to admit that a tiny edge of fear was making its way into her brain.

"Better get moving. I'd hate to be stuck in here overnight. Can't imagine any bears or wolves or wild dogs taking good care of me, gathering around for a little social time." She chuckled. "No Sneezy, Doc, or Sleepy to save me either."

She pushed her fears down and made herself continue.

In the distance, she could hear water. What a happy find. She could not only replenish her water supply, but also follow the stream to safety.

She had followed the stream for almost a half hour over rough terrain. At times, she was beside it and at other times high above it, looking down on it. If the forest were not so dense, she thought she could have seen where it led and gotten an idea of where she was, but no such luck.

Again, she rested. Now she wondered if she should have followed the stream in the other direction, but she had no energy for retracing her steps.

"I guess I have to admit defeat." She reached into the side pocket of her backpack for her cell phone. "Oh no, you didn't forget to put it in.

Damn it."

She thought over her preparations and remembered putting the phone in the backpack. She searched the pack thoroughly, and then her jacket and her jeans, knowing it wasn't there but just double-checking everywhere. Had it fallen out?

"Double damn. You stupid fool. This is getting to be a very expensive retreat."

She could feel the tears coming—a thing that rarely happened to her. But this was too much. Everything was closing in on her.

Forcing herself to get up and to move on, Lydia blew her nose and searched for some clue as to what she should do. Again, she determined that following the stream was the best choice.

Another ten minutes passed. She felt both physically and mentally weary.

Just ahead, maybe fifteen feet away, she saw something hatched into a tree. "Ah, a trail marking. Now I'm getting somewhere."

But it wasn't a familiar trail symbol. She studied it, tracing it with her fingertips, trying to understand it. Broken letters and numbers, just like the ones she'd found in the box. "Bryce did this?"

A low rumbling sound in the distance shook her from her numbness. A motor of some sort. Probably a truck, she guessed. "Can't be far from civilization now. I must be near either one of the side roads or the main road."

She moved toward the sound, which was waning, but she felt confident that she could find the road. She quickened her pace, almost to a run, but the density of the forest would not allow it for any length of time.

Scratched and sweating and physically exhausted, she soon came to the paved road. She sank down in the dirt on the shoulder. "I'm not moving. Someone will come along, and I'll beg a ride."

Leaning back against the bank at the side of the road, she began to drift into sleep. The sound of a vehicle approaching jerked her awake, and she struggled to get up. Her muscles were telling her she had taxed them far beyond their normal load.

It was her lucky day. Bryce pulled over and waited for her.

"Bryce, you can't know how happy I am to see you."

"What happened? You look beat."

"You've got that right. I got lost in the forest."

Bryce looked at her, and she could see his look of surprise followed by disdain.

"I know. It was stupid to take off without telling anyone and to think I could find my way without any aids."

"You mean you just took off walking?"

"I'm afraid that's the ugly truth."

"Where were you going?"

"I was coming to see you and Jan."

The look that crossed his face erased Lydia's feelings of relief.

John

John remembered that Josh had seemed excited about going kayaking, so he stopped at the rental place outside of Hollyville to check prices and times. Later he might buy his own kayak, especially if Lydia expressed an interest. It was hardly worth the purchase for just an occasional outing. He chose life preservers for both Josh and himself in a brilliant red that he knew was one of Josh's favorite colors.

At the grocery store, he purchased hamburger for grilling but no other meats. If he and Josh were lucky, they would catch some trout. At the vegetable stand on the highway outside of Hollyville, he stocked up on corn, tomatoes, and a watermelon.

He planned to let Josh help with the cooking. It was never too soon for children to learn their way around the kitchen. His own mother had insisted that he learn to do basic cooking, a skill that he had picked up again after Nancy's death. She had never wanted him in her domain, preferring that he have that time to relax. He smiled, remembering how she regularly tried new recipes, always eager to please him with different menus.

Back at the house, he checked the spare room again to see that everything was in place. Even though the room wasn't completely finished, it would do. At a yard sale he'd found a desk and reading lamp, and he had placed an armchair in one corner with a floor lamp. He would include a trip to the library so Josh could select books.

Keeping Josh busy would help keep his mind engaged and distracted from his troubles. He hoped he wouldn't have to pull him away from TV or video games, although he wasn't opposed to some viewing time. They could rent a couple of movies, if the weather turned bad, but mostly they would be outside hiking, camping, swimming, kayaking, and fishing—all the things he knew Josh would enjoy.

Friday arrived and he was ready.

He had just finished the salad preps when he heard a vehicle approaching. He took off his apron and stepped out on the porch.

His brother Neal carried the fishing gear, and Josh brought his bags from the trunk of the car. They exchanged greetings and handshakes.

"How about a beer, and there's lemonade for you, Josh." John pointed toward the cooler.

Neal opened a beer for himself and one for John.

"Ah, this sure hits the spot. Let's sit outside. I always forget what a prize view you have up here."

"You go ahead. I'll be right out as soon as I stir the stew."

"Mom's recipe?"

"You guessed it."

"Uncle John, I'm going down to the stream. Okay?"

"Sure, but first give yourself a spray." He pointed to the Cutters on the shelf near the door. "We'll call you for dinner in about twenty minutes."

"Water is a magnet for that boy. Guess it's in his blood. You and I never could stay away from it either. He told me on the way up that you might take him kayaking."

"Right. I checked into the rentals and bought a couple of life jackets for us."

"I thought you had some."

"They were all moldy and faded."

"Sounds like you've thought of everything."

"Well, yeah, I just want him to have a good time. How does he seem?

Handling things okay?"

"He's a good kid. Doesn't really complain, but I see some sadness in him. It digs deep into me, John. I wish to God I could have made my marriage work. It feels like I'll carry this pain for the rest of my life."

"I'm sorry, brother. How's Anne doing?"

"Fine, I guess. She's already got a new man around the house. Sure didn't take long for that to happen."

John heard the pain in his brother's voice. He reached for his shoulder. "Is Josh okay with that?"

"I don't know. I don't ask. I don't want to burden him."

"Sure. He'll let us know if anything is wrong."

"Maybe, but he's always been a quiet kid, just taking things in stride. I never know for sure what's going on in his head."

"But you'd know if he were really upset because he'd be acting out."

There was a pause.

"There is one thing."

John waited. He knew it was difficult to reveal what his brother considered his own personal failure.

"He wets the bed. Not all the time though."

"Well, that happens. Don't worry. I won't make a big deal out of it."

"He's good about it. Strips the bed and puts the sheets in the washer and makes up his bed fresh. I know it hurts him. I told him not to worry, but it doesn't seem to help."

"It will pass. That's really good that you aren't scolding him."

Neal sniffed and wiped at his eyes. John put his arm across his brother's shoulders.

"Thanks for keeping him. I know he'll have a blast up here. It's all he's talked about since you invited him. But a whole week, are you up for that?"

"You bet. He's good company."

Josh called to them, "Look who I found." He carried the Maine Coon cat in his arms. "I think we'll have to take Scrappy with us when we go fishing, Uncle John."

They all laughed.

※

After his shower, Josh came downstairs to John's office.

"So here you are, Scrappy." Josh dropped to the floor beside the cat.

"He comes in here every night about this time for his nightly brushing. Would you like to do it tonight?"

"Sure."

John pulled open the bottom drawer of his desk and handed the brush to Josh. "He likes a little extra pressure at the top of his head for some reason."

The boy brushed carefully, and John could hear the strong purring.

"Care for a bedtime snack? Some milk and a cookie?"

"Sounds good. Is it okay if Scrappy gets a snack?"

"Sure thing. You remember where I keep the cat food?"

"Yep. Come on, Scrap."

"I'll meet you upstairs in about ten minutes, Josh. We'll have a bedtime story, if you'd like one."

"Cool."

John smiled thinking about the sweet nature of this boy. It was comforting to have him in the house, spreading his enthusiasm and warmth.

※

John sat down on the edge of the bed facing Josh. "What kind of story shall we have?"

"Something a little scary but not too scary?"

"Sounds good. Here we go. Once upon a time in the North Carolina mountains, there lived a boy and his ferocious cat, Scrap. They liked to hang out together, to go searching around the woods for adventure, and to go hunting or fishing. The boy told everyone that Scrap was the best hunter in the entire world, far better than any hunting dog could ever be. And when he told people that, Scrap would puff up bigger and stronger than ever."

As if on cue, Scrap jumped up on the bed and circled around before nesting near Josh.

"One day, the boy and his cat were on their way to the stream to catch some fish."

"Uncle John, I'm the boy, right?"

"Do you want to be?"

John saw the hesitancy in Josh and waited.

"Okay."

John smiled. "Good. So they made their way through the woods and were almost at the stream when they heard crunching behind them. They turned around to see what it was, and what do you think was there?"

"A bear?"

"Exactly right. A big brown bear. Now this bear had not had much to eat that day, so he was especially hungry. He stood up on his hind legs and sniffed and sniffed the air and looked quite menacing. The boy began to worry.

"Even though he was a little bit scared, he did not show it. He decided he would be strong and brave. He turned to his cat and said, 'Scrap, let's invite the bear to go fishing with us.'

"Sure enough, Scrap led the way to the stream as if there was nothing to fear, and the big brown bear followed.

"When they got to the stream, the boy said, 'Mr. Bear, this is my cat, Scrap. He's going to catch some fish. And if you are very, very good, we will give you the fish.'

"Now the boy did not know if his plan would work, but he thought he had nothing to lose. And what do you think happened?"

"Scrap caught some fish and gave them to the bear."

"Exactly right. Tomorrow night, we'll see what happens next with the boy and his cat and the bear."

Josh smiled.

"Are you sleepy?"

"A little."

"Good. I'll sit here with you for a while. Shall we leave this small night light on for you?"

"Yes, please."

John rubbed the boy's head lightly for a moment and tucked the sheet and blanket around him gently.

"Good night, Josh"

"Night, Uncle John."

John stopped in the kitchen to pour a glass of wine before returning to his office. He settled into his swiveling chair and thought about Josh. He wondered what it would have been like if he and Nancy could have had children. *Don't go there. Just enjoy the boy. Maybe you can make a difference.*

Encounter with Bryce

Lydia hadn't expected to get lost, and she certainly hadn't expected Bryce to come along when he did. He said he'd take her to her house or to see Jan.

"I'd like to go to your house. Jan has told me how beautiful it is, and I'd love to see more of your work."

She noticed Bryce's stony countenance, but she reminded herself that she had never seen him display any warmth. If she waited for that to happen, she might never talk with him about his problems. Certainly, it was a risk. She could permanently alienate him, or worse, he could attack her. But if she could establish a link through art, it might be possible to reach him. She stretched out her legs and let out a sigh.

"I'm whipped. And I'm disgusted with myself for getting lost. I could really use a drink," she said.

"You won't get any booze at my house. I threw it out after the accident."

Lydia caught the tone in his voice. It was George Randolph who had told her Bryce's father had too much to drink before the accident. It hadn't occurred to her that a full-blown drinking problem was added into the mix. Was Bryce exaggerating? Even so, having an alcoholic parent would certainly cause additional trouble. These family problems could become so complicated. She felt all over again the weight of Jan and Bryce's situation.

"That accident was a terrible thing. You two were just kids at the time."

"We've managed."

She saw the tension in his shoulders and the hard grip on the steering wheel.

"Yes, but it's been hard for you."

"Planning on pulling some of that Lady Do-gooder stuff on us? We don't need it."

"You seem very angry, even after all of this time."

"Any reason why I shouldn't be angry?"

"Anger can be harmful to you and possibly to others. It can't be easy for Jan."

"Oh, I get it. She's been telling you a bunch of crap about me. Running over to your place for a daily gossip session."

"Not at all. I just notice that she seems to be afraid."

"Yeah? Afraid of what?"

"I don't know exactly. But I think it's not quite normal."

"Normal? You think you're a judge of normal?"

She paused, choosing her words carefully, "I think I am a good observer of behavior."

Bryce pulled the truck to a sudden stop. His arms were tense and his knuckles white from gripping the steering wheel. Sweat rolled down his face. He looked straight ahead.

"You don't know a damn thing about me and Jan, and you don't need to be butting your nose into our business."

"I'm sorry if I seem to be out of line, but I'm really just concerned."

"Nobody asked for your concern. Just leave us alone." His words sounded tortured.

"Bryce, I'm old enough, as I'm sure you're aware, to be your mother."

Tears streamed down Bryce's face, and he let his head fall forward on the steering wheel. She thought the word mother must have triggered the extra emotions. Should she comfort him?

She reached across the space and put a hand on his shoulder, fully expecting him to object, but he didn't. Wisely, she waited.

After a few moments, he pulled a handkerchief from his pocket, wiped his face, and blew his nose.

"Sometimes I think I'll explode, literally explode. I'm angry at everything and everybody. I hate it that I got adopted. What was wrong with me that my real mother didn't want me?"

"You can't be sure that she didn't want you. She may simply have wanted to do the best thing for you."

"Right. So I end up with a drunk for a father and a mother who doesn't care."

"I know things didn't turn out the way you wanted, but you have blessings surely."

"Jesus. Now you're going all religious. Preaching at me. You think that will help? Well, it won't."

"That did sound a little preachy, didn't it?" Lydia laughed. "The truth is, I work with students your age, but I don't have any children of my own. I don't have any real authority. I'm not a doctor or a counselor, just an art teacher. When I said you had blessings, I was thinking of your artistic talent."

Bryce was quiet now, as if all of his anger was spent.

"I was wondering, would you like to see some of my art? I'd like your opinion."

"My opinion," he scoffed.

"Yes, your opinion."

"I'm not a painter."

"True, but that doesn't keep you from having an opinion."

She wondered whether she should continue. There was no way of knowing what he was thinking or feeling. She waited.

"What do you want to know?"

She thought it an unusual question, but perhaps not so surprising, coming from a young person who doubted himself.

"I suppose I want to know whether my artwork speaks to you. I'm used to sharing my work with other artists, and we often give opinions about each other's work. It's satisfying to hear an informed person's thoughts."

"But I'm not an artist."

"You are. Most certainly, you are. Your boxes are of the highest quality. You cannot make me believe that you have no feelings or thoughts about other people's art."

"You have some paintings here?"

She thought she could see Bryce relaxing. Maybe there was a chance to reach him after all.

"I have my computer with photos of my work, and I have a few pencil drawings I've done since I arrived here."

"Jan's the one you want. She's always wanted to be an artist."

"She's told me. But she also knows you have exceptional ability. Have you thought about going to college?"

She saw the frown on his face, and wondered if she had gone too far too quickly.

"College is for other people."

"Why do you say that?"

"It just is."

"College is a place where you can meet lots of people and form friendships. Aren't you lonely?"

"I don't need anybody but Jan."

"I know you are very close, but that may change."

"I knew it. You're going to take her away from me. I hate you."

The change in his expression and his body was immediate and drastic. He put the truck in gear and hit the accelerator, spinning the wheels, causing Lydia to slide into the dashboard. He turned the truck around at the first available place and roared up the mountain toward Lydia's cabin.

Lydia sat in silence, frightened, admonishing herself for her stupidity. She searched for the right words, but nothing came. She wanted to escape, but she wasn't brave enough to risk a major injury by opening the door and jumping out. This wasn't a movie, but it was certainly a drama. A melodrama. She could only hope they would make it to the cabin. But then what would happen? She wouldn't let herself think about that.

"Bryce, slow down. We'll go over the edge if you aren't careful."

"Shut up. I know what I'm doing."

He tore around the curves, making the gravel fly. If someone came, there would be no stopping, and they would all roll down the mountain. She thought he wanted to crash, and nothing she could do or say would change his intentions.

But he didn't crash. He pulled into the parking slot and waited for Lydia to get out of the truck.

"Stay out of our business, or you'll be sorry." His voice cracked, and tears streamed down his face.

"Bryce, I didn't mean to interfere. I just wanted to help."

"You can't, so just leave us alone."

She walked up the path, climbed the few steps to the deck, and sank into the rocker. She grieved for the young man and for herself. She may have spoiled any chance of winning his trust.

Chance Meeting

Lydia pulled into the post office lot and parked next to a green Subaru. She wondered if it could be John's car. That would be a happy coincidence. They had left things unsettled the last time they spoke, only saying that they would get together soon.

Inside the post office, she saw John and Josh standing at the counter, adding stamps to a stack of envelopes. She noticed how comfortable they were with each other.

"My lucky day," John said when he noticed Lydia approaching.

"Mine too." She was struck by the warmth in his voice. "I hoped that might be your Subaru in the parking lot. In town for errands?"

John looked at his watch. "Yes, and it's about time for lunch. Care to join us at the local watering hole?"

"A splendid idea." She turned toward Josh. "Is that okay with you?"

"Yep. They've got great fish and chips. Almost as good as mine and Uncle John's." Josh high-fived his uncle.

"You've been cooking your own catch?"

John laughed. "Some, but we haven't caught the Big Guy yet. I told Josh the local legend about the trout that can't be caught, so now we're both determined to hook him."

"Sounds like fun and very much like a tall fish tale." Lydia winked at Josh.

"If we catch him, we'll let you help us cook him," Josh said.

Lydia laughed. She was charmed by this congenial young boy. "That's a deal, especially if you'll clean him."

"I can do that," Josh said, as he looked at his uncle.

"Absolutely." John handed the envelopes to Josh. "Want to post those for me? And then you can go stake out a spot for us at the café."

"Cool," Josh said.

John took Lydia's arm as they headed outside and down the street to Joe's Place.

"I can see that you two are having a fine time."

"He's an easy child, especially considering the circumstances."

"You mean the divorce. A tragic thing, but it happens so often now. The children must almost expect it."

"That doesn't mean it's easy."

"Definitely not, but it's possible for healing, especially if family members such as yourself step in to help. I admire you for doing that."

"Ah, some extra points for me. I'll take all you'll give me." He paused and turned toward her. "I'm really glad to see you."

They exchanged a long look, and Lydia felt excitement charge through her body. At the same time, she felt a tiny thread of worry. Would she make the right decision? So many times, she had come close to finding a soul mate, only to discover a potential problem that made her withdraw. Would it be different this time?

It was a pleasing hour over lunch. They compared notes on the recent storm, and John reported his progress on the house and made a date with Lydia to inspect it.

☙

Lydia took special care with preparations for her evening with John.

BLOCKED

She applied makeup with care and selected a sundress that made the most of her figure. A spray of White Linen cologne, her new dangly earrings purchased at the market, and she was ready.

She admitted to herself that she wanted John to like her as much as she liked him. *He's such a kind person, and he's wonderful with Josh.*

Still subdued from her recent encounter with Bryce, she needed to move out of herself and away from Jan and Bryce's problems, at least for this evening. She wouldn't abandon them, but clearly, some detachment would be a good thing.

She heard the approaching vehicle and soon after, the slam of the car door. She picked up her purse and a lightweight shawl before moving to the porch to greet John.

He whistled when he saw her. "Lovely. All this effort for me?"

"No, it's for Josh," she joked.

"No, it has to be for me. Josh went home today."

He came up the steps and reached for her. It was a gentle embrace and a light kiss, but enough for Lydia to know that she wanted more, if things continued to go right.

"A glass of wine?"

"A fine idea, but I have everything ready for us at the house, so if it's all right, we'll save your wine for another time."

They drove down the mountain, the windows open, the early evening coolness flowing around them, and the night sounds commanding attention. Lydia loved the freedom of not having to concentrate on driving, of being able to look into the forest to see the last rays of sun breaking through the pines in a few spots.

"We should have a remarkable sunset this evening at the lookout and at my place. I think I've timed it so we can catch it."

"How romantic."

"Is it? I suppose it is, but I've come to think of it as part of my daily dose of contentment, observing the gifts of nature."

"You really love it up here."

"Always have and always will. And you?"

"It's beautiful, and yes I like it, but I don't know if I'd want to live here year-round."

John turned to glance at her. "Rejecting me already, then?"

She laughed. "Surely, you're not thinking, 'love me, love my house.'"

"I'd be crushed if you didn't like my house with its fantastic view."

"Then I'm sure I will."

"So I don't have to feel defeated. Yet."

"Definitely not."

"Better. Much better."

They drove on in silence for a few moments. Lydia thought about Josh.

"Did the entire visit go well with Josh?"

"Yes, it did. No signs of problems that I could see. My brother told me Josh has been wetting the bed, but it didn't happen here."

"Being away from home probably helped. He could forget his anxiety."

"Something like that. He loves the outdoors and all that goes with it as much as I do, and we kept a tight schedule of activities."

"Sometimes that works for me."

"Yes? Meaning?"

"Meaning, I have felt some relief while being here, but I don't know if I've actually solved anything."

"You mean about your painting?"

"My painting and what I want to do with the rest of my life. I've become jaded about academe."

"The paperwork?"

"Partly, but it's more than that. Actually, I love teaching, being able to help young people hone their skills and develop a direction. It's just that I've begun to doubt my own artistic ability. It's as if I'm all used up. And maybe it wouldn't bother me so much if I'd had to deal with a dry spell before, but it's all new."

"It's probably a common problem. Have you talked with any of your colleagues about it?"

Lydia knew he meant to offer help, but it rubbed her the wrong way.

"Oh God, I can see I have some teaching to do right here. John, artists do not go around revealing to their competition that they've got a problem. Really, how can you even think that? You're an architect and a contractor. Can you see yourself announcing to your colleagues that you're in trouble?"

"Hey, wait a minute. Don't go ballistic on me. I didn't mean any harm."

Silence.

They both began to speak at the same time, and they laughed.

"Let me try that again. Okay, Lydia?"

She smiled. He didn't know that he was treating her delicately, as if she might break, not such a terrible thing. She knew her outbreak had caused it—his sensitivity would not allow him to behave otherwise.

He put his arm across the back of the seat and pulled her closer.

"There, that's better."

"Definitely better."

"Now if you want to tell me about this art thing that you're suffering through, please do, but if you'd rather not, that's fine too. Deal?"

"Deal. I do want to talk about it. I mean I want you to know what is bothering me. If we're to be good friends, or even more than friends, I hope we can always be honest in the big things."

"That's good—being honest in the big things. You'll never want me to tell you that you look terrible in an outfit, I think?" He pulled a big grin.

"Exactly right. But I will want you to tell me if I'm making a mistake or if I'm causing you pain."

"I can't imagine that you would do that, dear Lydia, certainly not intentionally, but I understand your meaning."

"Should we set this topic aside for now?" she asked.

"We can, if that makes you more comfortable. We can always try again later."

Lydia liked the fact that John was not afraid to talk about something as serious as what she wanted from life. She decided he was blessed with a healthy measure of self- confidence, but not arrogance. Impressive. She had recognized years ago that a lack of confidence usually guaranteed trouble for all involved.

Jan and Bryce Argue

Jan lounged on the front porch where the view always pleased her; the expanse of mountains in the distance created layers of blues, greys, and black above the forest line. She sipped her hot coffee slowly and let her mind wander.

To think that in a few months, she would be a college student! She wished it could be sooner. Today wouldn't be too soon. But she wanted to prepare Bryce for the change, even hoped that she would be able to convince him to join her. It would take some time to do that, more time than these few final weeks of summer. If Bryce got involved in courses, especially studio classes, he wouldn't need her, and their lives could finally take a more normal path.

She was jerked from her reverie by the sound of Bryce's truck pulling into the drive and the hard slam of the door a few seconds later.

"Jan?" he yelled. "Jan, where are you?"

She heard the anger in his voice and felt the familiar ache in her temples. She thought for a moment about slipping out the back door to avoid him. His moods were so annoying and lately frightening. But she went to the kitchen to meet him, planning to offer him some coffee, perhaps to calm him.

"What is it? You seem angry."

"Angry? Damn right, I'm angry. Why not, when everybody is accusing me of it, even you!" he yelled.

"Wait a minute, Bryce. What happened?"

"That bitch friend of yours, that's what happened."

She waited.

"You know who I mean. That fancy do-gooder artist you've been visiting all the time."

"Miss Lydia?"

Bryce mimicked Jan's words, as if he wanted to be sure his sister joined him in his anger.

"I don't understand you at all, Bryce. She's done nothing wrong. She's only tried to help."

"Help? Messing around in our business, you call that help?"

Jan saw the anger in his eyes and the sweat forming on his brow.

"You need to calm down, Bryce. Come on, you know you can tell me what's bothering you."

"I told you to stay away from her. Why didn't you listen?"

She reached for a mug and poured coffee for Bryce, stirred sugar into it, and offered it to him.

His eyes blazed with anger and disgust. He knocked the mug from her hand, sending the hot coffee across the counter and down her leg.

She jumped and shouted, "What the hell? What's wrong with you?"

"As if you didn't know. I'm sick of being dumped. Dumped by my own mother. Dumped by a boozing dad. And now dumped by you."

Jan grabbed a kitchen towel, ran cold water on it, and patted her leg until she felt relief. She turned back toward Bryce, ready to plead with him to listen to her, but he turned, crashing through the door and outside to the studio.

It would do no good to follow him to the studio when he was in this state of mind. She'd talk with him later. She couldn't imagine what had happened, but she meant to find out. She could either drag it out of Bryce, or she could ask Miss Lydia. She eased out the door and into the woods.

Lydia sat on the couch with her computer in her lap, viewing pictures of her work. She wanted to find some to show Bryce; not too many; that would overwhelm him. She'd decided not to let his adolescent behavior get to her, believing he wanted someone to care. Anyway, it wasn't in her nature to give up easily. This young man was crying for help, and she intended to help him find it. *Yes, Charles, I hear you. There are people trained to do this, but he just needs a push in the right direction.*

Completely absorbed in her thoughts, she didn't hear Jan's arrival.

"Miss Lydia, hello. Are you busy?"

Lydia looked up to see Jan standing on the porch.

"Come in, Jan. I was just preparing a file of my work. Maybe you'd like to see it."

It was then that Lydia noticed the tension in Jan and the look of fear on her face.

"Is something wrong, Jan?"

"It's Bryce."

"I'll make tea for us, and you can tell me about it."

Lydia selected mugs from the cabinet and a package of tea bags.

"Let's try Raspberry Cheer. You look like you could use some cheering up."

Lydia smiled at Jan, but Jan kept her frozen expression. "I think I may know something about this."

Jan twisted the end of her shirttail into a knot. "I thought you might."

Lydia noticed the release in Jan's voice and thought, not for the first time, *This young woman is a slave to her brother.*

Lydia asked, "Did Bryce mention me?"

"Yes, but he was so angry, he couldn't tell me what had happened. He stormed off to the studio, his usual trick."

Lydia noted the trace of anger in Jan's words. *Good. You need to be angry.* "And you were afraid to ask him?"

Jan looked away for a moment.

"I'm not surprised. He *is* filled with anger, and I told him so. I said it must be hard for you, for both of you, actually. And he blew up at me for interfering."

A look of recognition passed over Jan's face, and she told Lydia what had happened with the coffee.

"He's becoming more violent, and it's frightening me. I used to be able to calm him down, but lately—I just don't know."

Jan took a tissue from her pocket and wiped her eyes.

Lydia sighed. "I had hoped I could reach him though art, but maybe this has gone further than I thought. Are you afraid to be with him? Do you want to stay with me for a few days?"

Lydia saw relief in Jan's eyes, but Jan shook her head.

"He'd be even more angry if I stayed away, and I don't know what he might do."

"But you are not responsible for his behavior, Jan. You have a right to protect yourself both physically and emotionally."

"Don't you see? I'm all he has. I have to help him, to protect him from himself. I can't just blow him off. Something terrible might happen."

"Oh my dear, you are such a good sister, so generous and kind. But Bryce needs more than you can give him. He needs the counseling you and I talked about before. Maybe I'll have a chance to guide him toward that, but right now I want you to be safe."

Jan stood up. "I'll be okay. Promise. But I'd better go before he comes looking for me."

Lydia reached for Jan's hands and held them. "Are you sure you won't stay?"

"No, I'd just be worrying. I'm sure Bryce will be cooled down by now and probably feeling sorry, so I'll be able to talk with him."

Lydia stood and walked with Jan to the door. "Maybe I should go with you."

"No. I'll be fine. Thanks for listening." Jan stopped at the bottom of the porch steps. "I'm sorry to be such a bother, Miss Lydia."

"You're not a bother, not at all. Don't worry. We'll get this worked out."

Lydia saw the childlike trust in Jan, and it worried her.

"Let me drive you home."

"No, it's better this way. Walking through the woods always puts things right for me. Please don't worry."

Charles Visits Lydia

Charles felt he'd more than earned a vacation after teaching the long summer session—not the easiest or most fascinating group of students, and that, combined with the hottest summer on record, made him eager to drive to the mountains.

It felt good to leave his usual school costume behind in exchange for a pair of lightweight khakis, his favorite blue checked sport shirt, and his classic Italian loafers. He packed an overnight bag and set off after lunch, knowing he had plenty of time for a leisurely drive to Hollyville. He would arrive in time for cocktails, just as Lydia had suggested.

He turned the radio to the FM station and listened to a spirited rendition of *The Magic Flute*, one of his favorite operas. *The Queen of the Night* did not disappoint him, nor did the trio of young boys. Through the years, he'd heard too many productions where both were lacking.

A few hours later, at the Hollyville florist, he selected a bouquet of red roses, pink carnations, and orange Shasta daisies.

"Is there a wine shop in town?"

The pretty young woman, he guessed was in her twenties, directed him to the grocery store.

"You're going to make someone happy," she said.

"That's the idea." Charles smiled. "Is the Market open today? The friend I'm visiting told me you have a Market on the weekends."

"Yes, just continue down Main Street to the park. You'll see it."

"Good." He turned to leave but had a second thought. "Do you know the work of a young man who makes boxes? I believe his name is Bruce, or maybe it's Bryce Johnson?"

"That would be Bryce Johnson. He makes beautiful wooden boxes and sells them at the Market."

"Thank you, young lady, you've been most helpful."

Charles checked his watch. Plenty of time to swing by the Market. He parked around the corner and found Bryce's stall easily, but not Bryce. Instead a very pretty blonde girl greeted him.

"What extraordinary craftsmanship."

"Yes, my brother makes them."

He noticed the pride in her voice.

"And you're minding the stall for him?"

"Just for a while. He'll be back soon if you want to talk with him."

"No, that won't be necessary. I'd like to purchase this one with the leaf carvings. It's especially fine." He turned it over, looking for a price.

"That will be sixty dollars, please."

Charles extracted the bills from his wallet and handed them to her.

"Shall I wrap it for you? It won't take long."

"Please."

He watched as she took a square of brown paper, placed the box in the center, and expertly folded and taped the ends before adding a narrow black satin ribbon.

"Beautifully done. Please tell your brother how much I admire his work. And now I'd like to see your work too."

He saw the look of surprise in her eyes.

"Oh, I can explain. My friend Lydia Drexel told me about the artwork you and your brother sell here at the Market. She told me you do very nice miniature scenes."

"Oh, I see. You're visiting Miss Lydia."

BLOCKED

At that moment, Bryce entered the back of the stall.

"Bryce, this is a friend of Miss Lydia's. He's just bought one of your boxes."

Charles extended his hand and introduced himself, but Bryce kept his head lowered and failed to return the courtesy. "You do excellent work."

"It's something to do."

"It's more than that, and I think you know it."

Charles watched the youth, wanting to see if Lydia's assessment was accurate. Handsome and cocky but not interested in people. He couldn't tell much more in this short time.

"I was just asking your sister about her art. Will you show me, Jan?"

Jan led the way to her stall where Charles examined and commented on the work. He selected one for purchase and chatted for a few minutes before going to his car. As he drove to Lydia's cabin, he thought about Jan and Bryce. Such handsome youth. He wondered if Lydia had let her sense of drama lead her astray.

At the cabin, he found Lydia in the kitchen preparing a plate of cheese and olives to go with the glasses of wine that she poured.

He handed her the flowers and wine.

"Charles, always so thoughtful." She gave him a brief hug. "Inside or outside?"

"Outside. I'll carry the wine and nibbles. You bring this." He handed her the bag Jan had given him.

"There's more?"

"Certainly. All for my charming hostess."

Lydia knew as soon as she saw box-shapes wrapped in brown paper. "You went to the Market."

"I wanted to check out your dysfunctional kids. I have to say that other than Bryce being a little antisocial, I saw nothing amiss. Are you sure you haven't dreamed this drama up, Lyd?"

Lydia frowned. "Give me some credit. You were with them for all of ten minutes?"

"Right. And I admit I wasn't peeling away the sociological or psychological layers." He winked at Lydia.

"If you'd heard and seen all that I've seen, you'd think differently."

"So. You're still convinced that there's some deep, dark mystery between these two?"

"I'm positive that Jan needs to escape the hold her brother has on her. Whether it's his fault or hers or both, I can't say conclusively, but family circumstances play a role."

Before they could go into further discussion, a car approached.

"More guests?"

"None planned."

A couple of moments later, John appeared on the path.

"I apologize, Lydia. I was in the area and decided to stop by. I should have called."

"Please, it's no problem. Come meet my friend Charles."

She made introductions and offered her rocker to John. "I'll get you a glass of wine."

"Thanks, that would be great."

Charles saw immediately why Lydia was attracted to this handsome, self-assured man, not that he liked the idea. But for Lydia's sake, he would force himself to be gracious.

"Lydia has told me about the house you're building. It sounds fantastic, especially the view."

"I can't deny that. It was the view that sold the lot, and I've tried to design a house worthy of the view."

"Lots of glass?"

"Glass and a wraparound deck."

Lydia returned with the wine for John and took a seat on the wide porch rail. But both men stood and offered their seats to her.

She laughed. "Please sit down, both of you. I'm quite comfortable here."

There was a moment of silence.

"Charles has been my friend, actually my mentor, for years at the college. He's saved me from scrapes and counseled me on the ways of academe endlessly."

"You make me sound like a tiresome old bore, my dear."

Lydia laughed and John saved the moment by raising his glass.

"A toast to friendship and a special tribute to mentors."

Lydia Poses New Questions

Lydia packed up her laptop; she could show Bryce more of her work if he seemed interested.

Stepping onto the sun-drenched porch, she paused to watch the hummingbirds darting back and forth, bombarding one another, taking a few sips from the feeder and then whooshing away into the forest and back again. Such an appealing sight. She vowed to purchase a feeder for her deck at home.

Home. Only a few more weeks and she would return to her small house in its cul-de-sac in a quiet section of town, only a few blocks from Spring Valley College. There was nothing architecturally remarkable about the traditional bungalow, but under her artistic hand, it had become a jewel. Collected memorabilia, baskets from the Southwest, glass from Italy, and sculpture from a fellow artist, artfully and sparingly arranged, provided accents that complemented her paintings.

She remembered Charles remarking that her house made him feel like he was walking into a painting. He'd said the details blended into a pleasing composition; the colors were subtle and yet commanding in their unity, each arrangement demanding thoughtful examination—all of the pieces coming together to make a finished picture that welcomed him.

In that moment, Lydia missed her house. She wanted to walk around it and through it, soak it up, and revel in its special comforts.

Her mind turned to her studio at the back end of the house, an addition she'd designed and contracted to have built before she moved into the house, over a dozen years ago. She could imagine herself sitting in her rocker in front of the easel, focusing on a blank canvas. Just for a second, she felt the old itch—the need to express her thoughts and feelings on that clean white surface; it had been a place of challenge and of comfort, and she believed it would be again.

She wondered if John would like her house. If things continued to progress, it wouldn't be long before she invited him to visit her studio. If they decided to be a couple, would they live in her house or his? Would she continue to teach? So many new questions to consider.

Every time she and John were together, she felt more certain that she wanted to be with him on a more permanent basis. She still wondered if she were ready for marriage. After all of these years alone, the prospect of giving over so much of herself and her time scared her. She hadn't expressed these thoughts to John, at least not concretely. She knew it was essential. *I'll bring it up the next time I see him. Probably on our hike this weekend.*

But right now, she wanted to work with Bryce. She couldn't leave this young man stranded, engulfed in his periods of uncontrolled anger, a threat to himself and to his sister. And she understood the codependence in Jan and Bryce's relationship; if she worked with one, she must also work with the other, get both of them to Spring Valley where she could be a contact for them.

All those years watching her sister deal with her mental illness had left a mark. For so long, she couldn't accept the fact that her sister wouldn't get well. Such a strange illness, so elusive. When the drugs worked—no, correct that—when her sister took the drugs consistently, she seemed normal. Her sense of humor returned, and she could focus on her work and friendships, but as soon as she stopped taking them, everything fell apart again. She became paranoid about people and their motives, which led to distrust all around.

Was Bryce experiencing some of the same tendencies? It didn't seem so. Anger was his biggest problem. She still wasn't sure what caused it, but if only she could get him into a more normal environment, into art courses and into some friendships, she felt confident that he could move ahead.

And Jan definitely needed to go to college, wanted to go. There was nothing for her in this isolated place.

She walked down the steep path, breathing in the woodsy fragrance and the scent of pine each time she brushed against a branch or stepped on the pine straw.

It was a good morning to walk, but she was eager to contact Bryce, so she decided to drive. The fact that she had gotten lost still rankled her. But then there was the surprise gift of finding the carving in the tree. Again, she wondered about the connection between the symbols. She expected there to be an answer eventually.

After turning onto the Johnson's road, in a few short minutes, she came to the rustic rock wall that framed the curving driveway leading to the house. Clusters of vines and bushes draped their tendrils over the wall, softening its edges. After another hundred yards, the sprawling stone house with its wraparound porch came into view. Several rockers sat at angles, as if forming a ring, ready for conversation. Lydia imagined how once this family had entertained their guests on the porch, the woods forming a protective bower, the mountain rising above the trees in the distance.

She parked beside Bryce's truck, picked up her satchel with the laptop, and walked toward the front door, but at the last moment, she took the path around the house toward the studio. She heard recorded strains from an unfamiliar ballad and concluded it must be Bryce's choice of music. Through the screen door, she could see him sitting on a stool, bent over a piece of wood, working a lathe to cut away excess wood. Ribbons of the wood peeled away and dropped to the floor, forming a rich brown sea at his feet.

She tapped firmly on the side of the screen door. "Good morning."

Bryce turned, placed the wood on his workbench, and came to greet Lydia.

"I didn't think you'd come."

He held the door open for her and motioned her toward a couple of Adirondack chairs in one corner of the room.

"You didn't think I wanted to see your work?" she asked.

"Something like that."

She realized that once again she had the task of drawing him out. She had hoped she could continue from where they had left off yesterday, that it would be easier. She chided herself for her lack of patience.

"That looks like an interesting new piece. I don't think it's a box though."

"Nope. I like to work with figures and animals and birds when I need a break from boxes."

Lydia was surprised when he handed her the piece of wood. She interpreted it as an offering, a gesture of trust.

"I sometimes get an idea for a piece just by holding the wood and examining the grain and feeling its weight."

She turned the wood, one way and then another, sniffed its fragrance, and traced the grain with her fingertips.

"Does it remind you of anything?" he asked.

"Not an object, no." She held it to her nose again. "I love the fragrance."

"Do you know what it is?"

"You mean like maple or walnut or oak?"

"Yeah."

"I'll take a guess. Maple?"

"Right. Plenty of that around here. I've always liked it, even though it's not rare, like say ebony. I've never understood why people put so much value on the so-called rare woods anyway."

Lydia noticed the gradual change in Bryce. It made sense: he was in his own territory surrounded by his creations. He was the teacher now, offering his knowledge.

"Do you know what it's going to be?" she asked.

He surprised her again when he smiled. It felt like a rare gift. It turned him into a new person, confident and handsome.

He took the wood from her, cradled it in his hands, and said, "It's a surprise."

"Something for Jan?"

He didn't answer.

Lydia drew in her breath deeply. She hoped she hadn't spoiled the mood. She understood what Jan had meant; as long as he was engaged in his art, he was calm. Art was his escape. *Just like it has been for me.*

She stood and walked around the room. It was a modest but good space: two long benches placed at right angles, a tool peg-board above each of the benches, shelves and cabinets for storage, and a line of narrow windows near the ceiling on the north wall. Three skylights added enough natural light, but she noted Bryce had a high-intensity lamp, probably for his finely detailed work and possibly for late-night work. Probably he came to his studio, just as she went to hers, at those moments in the night when a new idea came or when sleep refused to come.

Looking at a display of boxes and small, beautifully detailed birds and animals, Lydia felt the power of these well-crafted objects.

"All of these are simply exquisite, Bryce. They are more than a likeness. Expressive. Unique. I feel your reverence for nature in them."

She picked up a delicate hummingbird. Its tiny wings were finely carved, the layers of feathers stacked and tapered perfectly. Its stance gave her the feeling of the tiny creature's quest.

"I don't remember seeing these on display at the Market."

"Nope."

"Is there a reason?"

"Too many hours in them. I'd have to charge more than people'd want to pay."

"Have you tried?"

"Nope. Not going to either."

She felt again that he was slipping away. Such complexity in him. Was he afraid of competition, or was it fear of rejection that made him keep this part of his art private? Maybe it was none of that. Maybe he didn't need to compete. His sense of achievement and pleasure came simply in the act of creation.

She walked over to the workbench and stood closer to him. She watched him working with the lathe.

"Do you mind if I stand here?"

"Do *you* mind if people watch *you* work?"

She paused to collect her thoughts, and the silence continued for a few moments.

"Well, would you mind if I watched you work?" he asked again.

Lydia realized no one had ever watched her paint; well, not since art school, when her studio professor had walked around the room, pausing to watch first one student and then another. She'd never been a *plein air* or street-painter but instead had closeted herself in the comfort of her studio.

Bryce chuckled.

"I suppose I have to admit that you've cornered me, Bryce."

"Not intentionally. I just thought it was kind of funny for you to ask when you're already doing it. I don't guess I'd let you come in here if I was afraid to have you watch me work."

Lydia noticed his emphasis on fear. Maybe that was the right feeling. Would she be afraid to let someone she barely knew watch her paint? Or would she be afraid to let someone she knew, say John, watch her paint? She tried to imagine herself painting with someone watching each brush stroke, each new choice of color.

"I'm baffled by your thinking that fear would be involved."

"Who said anything about fear?"

She paused, wondering if she wanted to push this.

He repeated, "What about fear?"

"I must have misunderstood you."

More silence.

Bryce walked to the corner of the room and took a chunk of wood from the storage bin. He handed it to Lydia.

She held it, turned it, and sniffed it. "Nice."

Bryce handed her the lathe. "Want to try your hand at this?"

Momentarily baffled, she looked at his face. "You want me to carve something?"

"You can try it. You might like it."

"I might, but I hardly know where to begin."

"Just start, and see what the wood tells you. Eventually, something will come to you. If you need help, you can ask me."

"And what if I mess up this perfectly good piece of wood?"

"Nothing ventured; nothing gained."

Lydia laughed.

After turning the wood one way and another for a few moments, she decided she might as well go ahead. The first strips fell away, and the fragrance of the wood intensified. It felt right and good.

"There, that's good, but hold the lathe this way, and you'll have more control. Work it away from you, instead of toward you for now."

She followed his instructions. "Ah, right. That's easier."

"Bryce, I want to tell you something."

Silence.

"Well, I guess you'd better tell me." He paused. "If you haven't changed your mind. Being a woman, I suppose that's your right."

Lydia laughed again. She liked these moments when Bryce's sense of humor surprised her.

"Just think. I came here with the idea of asking you if you'd like to try painting, but here I am trying your craft."

"I used to paint in art classes in high school, but I never liked it. It never felt natural for me."

"Maybe I could show you some methods that have worked for my students and for me."

He turned to her. His expression was difficult to read. Curiosity, mistrust, or both?

"Why are you doing this?" he asked.

Lydia paused, worried that she had taken the wrong approach. If she were working in the studio with her students, she would not have been so tentative.

At that moment, Jan opened the screen door to the studio.

Lydia Struggles with the Triangle

Jan toweled her long blonde mane until it was almost dry. Rarely did she use a dryer unless she wanted to style her hair. On hot, humid days, she tied it into a ponytail for comfort, but on a day like this one, she let it flow around her face and across her shoulders.

Any artist would cherish her as a model. Her sculpted facial features were complemented by the golden halo of wavy hair and her lean, lithe body was flexible enough to twist itself into numerous appealing stances.

She remembered that Miss Lydia had told her she would be a good model, that she could earn some pocket money modeling for the art department at Spring Valley. Models were always in demand, especially good ones.

She pulled on jeans and a sweatshirt, slipped into her moccasins, and walked outside to the studio.

She heard voices. Stepping closer to the door, she saw Bryce talking to Lydia.

Jan watched her brother and Lydia from the edge of the door, out of their view. Bryce stood in front of a row of his carved animals, and Lydia held a piece of wood, stroking it and then sniffing it. She then picked up the lathe and cut into the wood.

Both seemed relaxed. Jan shook her head as if trying to shake away unwanted feelings, opened the door, and walked toward the long workbench where Lydia and Bryce stood.

Jan put a smile on her face. "Miss Lydia. I didn't know you were here. Did you walk? I guess you didn't get lost this time," she joked.

"I drove. I'm surprised you didn't hear me arrive."

"I must have been in the shower."

Jan walked around Bryce and placed herself on the other side of Lydia. They formed a triangle—Bryce at his workbench, Jan on one side, and Lydia on the other.

"I came to see more of Bryce's work," Lydia said.

"I thought you wanted to see the house," Jan said.

Lydia turned toward Jan, to have eye contact. "Oh, I do, but when I heard the music coming from the studio, I came here first, thinking I might find both of you here."

After a moment of silence, Lydia continued, "I hadn't realized your brother made anything but boxes."

"Just like I told you. He's the talented one," Jan said.

Bryce turned toward Jan. "Why do you do that?"

"What?"

"You know what I mean. Always setting me up as special. Like you don't count. You know I hate that."

Jan waited for a moment before responding. "Miss Lydia knows you have talent."

"So?"

Jan shook her head, sending the blonde strands flying out from her face. She stepped closer to her brother and reached for his hand. "I was praising you, but you make me sound stupid. Why do you do that?"

Bryce turned toward Lydia. "Dr. Drexel, maybe you can get some sense into her. Make her stop putting herself down all the time."

Uncomfortable silence continued.

Bryce immediately turned back to his work. Jan looked out the window, and Lydia looked at first one and then the other, as if evaluating the situation.

"Now look what you've done. Miss Lydia is our guest, and you're making her upset."

"Yeah? It's always me. I'm always the bad guy. Right, Jan?"

"No, I didn't mean that. You're always getting everything I say and do wrong," Jan snapped.

Bryce continued his carving.

"Would you like a cup of tea, Miss Lydia? I could show you the house."

Lydia thought Jan's voice sounded plaintive.

Before Lydia could respond, Bryce strode across the room to Jan's section of the studio. He held up a drawing. "What do you think this is if it isn't talent? Stop hiding behind me, Jan. Stop manipulating everything and everybody." He dropped the drawing on the drafting table and returned to his workbench.

Lydia had only a brief glimpse of the drawing, a mountain scene with a wide border of intertwined figures circling it. She wasn't sure, but wasn't something about the border vaguely familiar?

Lydia walked across the room to examine the drawing. While she stood looking at it, Jan rushed forward and snatched the drawing away.

"No, it's not finished."

"Oh, I'm sorry. I didn't know. I should have asked."

Bryce said, "That's right. None of your drawings are ever finished. You keep them hidden in here. If you'd let me frame them, we could sell them at the Market."

"They're not good enough." Jan paused. "They're not finished. And anyway, what about you, keeping your carved figures hidden?"

"That's totally different, and you know it."

Lydia sensed the tension rising and felt compelled to mediate. "I can solve this little dispute easily," she said as she stepped closer. "You both have talent, and I want both of you to come to Spring Valley College where you can develop your talent further."

"Cut the college crap. I'm not going," Bryce snarled.

Lydia instinctively pulled back from Bryce. "I didn't mean to dictate your future, Bryce. I was only trying to make a sensible suggestion."

"Okay, so I'm not sensible." Bryce's voice lost its anger.

Lydia reached out and put her hand on his shoulder. "Quite to the contrary, Bryce. You've found a way to use your talent to solve your personal problems. That's not only admirable but enviable. As an artist, I've found myself in the same place at times."

Bryce scoffed. "You think you understand, but you don't."

Lydia paused, uncertain of what she should say, but she was determined to take advantage of the moment. "I *know* something is troubling you. Both of you, and I'd like to know what it is so that I might help in some way."

"That again."

"Yes, that again. Please trust me. Let me help you."

Jan stood looking at her brother.

Lydia could see the anger in Jan's eyes.

"I've had it with you, Bryce! You're making me crazy, always following me around and giving me trouble. I'm fed up. I'm going to college, and you can just stay here."

Lydia felt pulled one way and then another, first by Bryce and then by Jan. Her natural reaction was to try to mediate, to be the classroom teacher in charge, to bring some kind of resolution. But what would work best?

Bryce turned away from them, picked up the piece of wood, and resumed carving.

Lydia saw that he was returning to his comfort zone, immediately absorbed in the work before him.

Suddenly, she realized that if she had a canvas in front of her, she would fill it with boiling colors and rolling motions. Without a canvas, her medium had to be words. But what words?

Or she could simply leave.

The idea brought a rush of freedom for a moment, but she never wanted to abandon a project. *A project. Such a demeaning way to think.* She shook herself mentally and decided to make one more effort.

She took Jan's hand and walked toward Bryce. "I want both of you to hear me out. Will you do that for me?"

Lydia's Plea

Thoughts swirled in Lydia's head. Jan's recent flash of anger toward her brother had given Lydia a new perspective. For weeks she had thought it was Jan who needed to be free from Bryce, but now she believed it was Bryce who needed that freedom.

She knew Jan responded to the outdoors, but Bryce felt best in the studio. A neutral place would work best for their talk, but her intuition would have to guide her to that place.

"It's such a pleasant day. Could we take a turn around the grounds and perhaps see the house before we get into the serious side of things?" Lydia said, as she looked first at Jan and then at Bryce.

Bryce raised his shoulders in distracted assent.

Jan's brow unfurled, and she sighed quietly.

They stepped outside, walked away from the studio, and wandered around the house on the winding paths through the flower gardens, talking about the variety of day lilies, the wildflowers, and the flowering ground cover and bushes. Each time Lydia saw something unusual, she stopped and asked for details. Both Jan and Bryce were knowledgeable, but it was Jan who took the lead.

"There are two types of rhododendron that line the lane coming down to the house. The Catawbas peak in June but hang on into July sometimes if we have the right amount of rain, and the Rosebays peak in July. You probably saw some of those on your way in. They're my favorite of the rhododendrons."

"I suppose you had those planted?"

"I'm not sure, but probably. Lots of them just grow wild and spread on their own, especially if conditions are right," Jan said. "Mom loved working in these beds. She grew up on a farm and knew a lot about plants and how to take care of them. She was always studying on the Internet about new plants—looking for ones that could survive here under the trees."

"So what's this little pink flower? It's so unusual." Lydia asked. She was surprised when Bryce responded.

"Pink turtleheads." He held one of them open so Lydia could see their shape. Then he showed her a bud that looked exactly like a turtle's head.

"And the design of the gardens, was that your mother's doing, too?" Lydia asked. "I love the graceful shapes of the beds, the way they curve around in interesting ways under all of these tall oaks, maples, and pines."

"I think they had somebody help with that, but we all worked out here together sometimes. Dad was proud of the house and the plantings and liked to tell people about it. Kind of bragged all the time. Right, Bryce?"

"I just remember that sometimes I had to help with the weeding, and I never wanted to do it, but then when it was done, I could go back to my art," Bryce said.

"When I worked out here with Mom, she and I talked about stuff, and that was so cool. She'd tell me about growing up on the farm and how different it was. She said her mother grew her flowers mostly along the edges of their big vegetable garden. Nothing formal at all, so that's probably why she liked our place so much."

"You felt close to her at those times?" Lydia asked.

"Well, yeah, cause, you know, it made me feel like I knew her better." Jan paused before continuing. "I really miss her."

Lydia heard the wistfulness in Jan's voice and was reminded of her feelings for own mother. "It's a sad thing to lose our parents. My mother

BLOCKED

died a few years ago, and like you, I continue to remember things we did together, and I still wish I could talk with her. That will probably never go away completely."

Bryce interrupted. "Could we move along? I need to get back to my carving."

Realizing Bryce might be uncomfortable with the topic, or that he might feel excluded, Lydia turned toward Bryce and asked, "Do you have lots of memories of your mother?"

"Sure, but I don't spend much time on them. My carving takes up my time."

"As it should. I understand completely."

They were near the side entrance to the screened porch, so Lydia proposed that they sit there in the rockers. When they were comfortably settled, Lydia began.

"I've thought so much about you two since I met you. The fact that we're all working with art made a connection for me. It was like an extra gift coming to the Market and seeing your fine work. And when you gave me one of your boxes, Bryce, I was so pleased."

Lydia watched Bryce for a reaction, but he kept his head down, as if waiting patiently for her to finish.

"You both know that I'm here for a holiday, but actually for more than that. I'd reached an impasse in my work. I'm totally blocked. After years of always having a sense of direction, of knowing what I wanted to do next, I suddenly was without any new ideas. I sat in my studio in front of a blank canvas with not a single notion of what I wanted to express. It made me feel tired and dreary. Even a little bit of panic, if I'm honest.

Bryce raised his head and looked at Lydia. She saw surprise in his eyes.

"I wonder if that has ever happened to either of you."

Bryce shook his head, no; Jan remained silent.

"Only recently have I begun to have a bit of zeal building inside me again, and I think I can thank you two for that gift."

Bryce began to rock steadily, but Jan continued to sit rigidly in her rocker.

"What are you getting at, Dr. Drexel?" Bryce asked.

Lydia smiled. "I do tend to take a long time to make a point, but that's probably because I want to be certain I do it the best way. Or maybe it's the teacher part of me."

"Going to paint portraits of us, are you?" Bryce asked in a joking way.

Lydia laughed robustly.

"I hadn't thought of it, but that's not a bad idea."

"Or maybe you'll open a woodworking shop?" Bryce grinned.

Lydia smiled. "Even though you set a fine example, it'll be a long time before I'm ready to do anything credible with wood. Still, with your instruction, who knows what I might achieve? Or what others might achieve if you decided to teach. I think you have a whole new world to explore beyond your own studio."

Jan stood suddenly and left the porch, letting the screen door slam behind her. She darted into the woods.

Lydia stood and moved toward the door after her.

"You might as well let her go. You won't be able to catch her."

Lydia turned to face Bryce.

"What do you think happened? I must have said the wrong thing."

Bryce didn't answer immediately. "She's like this when she gets upset."

"Do you want to talk about it?"

"Not particularly."

Bryce stood and moved toward the door. He mumbled, "There's nothing you can do."

BLOCKED

"Perhaps not, but I really want to help."

"No, you can't. It's like I told you before."

Bryce moved down the path toward the studio, and Lydia let him go.

Lydia Talks with John

Lydia kept wondering why Jan had left so abruptly.

She drove back to her cottage, thinking Jan might be there when she arrived, but she wasn't. She waited on the porch, looking into the woods to see if there was any indication of movement, any sign of Jan. Nothing.

It was almost lunchtime. She sliced cheddar cheese to go with a stack of crackers, blended fresh berries and yogurt, and heated water for tea before returning to her favorite spot on the porch.

Her mind turned again to the border on Jan's drawing. Despite only a glimpse of the figures and shapes, Lydia believed they were connected to the message in the box and the carving on the tree. The symbols, according to the report Charles had sent, were related to Native American history as well as Greek mythology. What was Jan dabbling in? Could this be a connection to her temperament?

If Bryce had been willing to reveal more about Jan's behavior or his concerns, Lydia could have felt more secure in her observations. Whether the symbols were of importance or not, she believed Jan was more troubled than Bryce.

On a whim, Lydia decided to drive to John's, where with any luck, he would be working on the house. She felt an overwhelming need to be with him and to talk with him about these new concerns.

Twenty-five minutes later, she was driving up the steep, winding driveway to John's house. She saw his familiar green Subaru parked in the drive, and her heart lifted.

BLOCKED

She found him on the second floor hammering away, placing the molding around the ceiling in the master bedroom. He was so absorbed, she doubted he knew she was there.

"Hello!"

John let out a yelp. "Lydia! You scared me. Is everything all right?"

"Yes, I just had to see you. Can you come down off that ladder for a little while?"

He obliged her and surprised both of them with fervent kisses, which led to an initiation of the master bedroom. Right there among the tools, on the floor.

Twenty minutes later he said, "Can we make a habit of this? Please."

Lydia laughed and kissed him again, causing an additional delay of his work and of Lydia's second reason for being there.

Eventually, she pulled him out to the balcony to sit on the wide railing.

"I need to talk."

"Oh no, this sounds ominous."

"Not really. It's just that I'm entangled in the Johnsons, and I need some good advice from an intelligent, sensitive man."

John looked all around and over his shoulder.

She laughed, mimicked the Uncle Sam poster pose, and said, "I want you."

"I've been waiting for this important decision, in case you didn't know." He reached for her again and kissed her gently before continuing. "Okay. Shoot."

"An appropriate word for the situation. Right now, I'd like to shoot, figuratively that is, these two kids. I can't figure out what the hell is going on with them. First, I was sure Jan was being abused by her brother."

Lydia saw John's appalled look and backtracked. "No, I don't think that's happening, at least not physically."

"So it's the reverse? Bryce is being abused?"

"Maybe. In a way. I can't be sure."

"But you want to find out, and you want to help them. Right?"

"At the risk of sounding totally naïve, yes. Their problem has gotten into my head, and I can't get rid of it. It's just not right or normal for these two to remain holed up here in their semi-mansion, selling their work at the Market, and not getting on with life. They should both be in college."

"Whoa there. You're assuming that every person needs a college education."

"No, of course not. But I see two talented, intelligent youth who need to move on, and college is the sensible answer. It's quite obvious that their relationship is flawed. Probably they both need counseling to get past their parents' accident, if nothing more. But actually they need much more, and they can get that while in college. We have a wonderful art program as well as all kinds of other programs to offer and a very successful counseling center at Spring Valley."

"And you think they'll walk in there and head straight for counseling?" John asked.

"I know it sounds crazy."

"An interesting word choice, if you don't mind my mentioning it, my dear."

"I know. It's all a little crazy."

"So what's the newest development? You seem to be particularly agitated."

Lydia told John about the last few sessions with Bryce that had made her think she was getting closer to him. She explained how she had been in their studio and had discovered Jan's hesitancy to show her work. She told him about the drawing with the mysterious border and about Jan's sudden retreat into the woods.

"And you think Jan is the one who's messed up?"

"I think there is something very wrong that Bryce has been keeping covered, and I think it's related to her artwork and the symbols she uses."

"What do you plan to do?"

"That's just it. I don't have a plan. I could just walk away. Nobody would expect me to try to solve these problems, but I can't do that. I suppose it comes partly from my years of working with youth, many of them troubled and looking for answers. I've been able to direct them to counseling, and part of it I'm sure relates to my sister's problems. I tried so hard for years to help her, but her illness was way beyond my skills. She had to be hospitalized eventually. And the disease affected her immune system so that she couldn't fight cancer, or at least that's what I think, and so she had an early death. It was all really heartbreaking and terrible for my parents and me."

John reached for her hand and held it firmly. His eyes never left her face. Lydia took in the comfort and let it envelop her.

"It's about this age, in their early twenties, when young people need help immediately. It's when schizophrenia most frequently occurs. With the new drugs and the better counseling services, there is more hope today. I might help them avoid going off the deep end."

"You think these kids are mentally ill?"

"I don't know if they are actually mentally ill, but I see real problems for them, and I think it's only going to get worse."

John left his perch on the railing and moved toward Lydia. He pulled her into his arms, held her, stroked her hair, and whispered, "I love you so much, Lydia."

Then he looked into her eyes. "But I don't want you to get hurt. I admire you for wanting to help, but I think this thing may be much too big."

"But if something happens to one of them or to both of them, I'll be devastated."

"No, darling, you won't. I'll be with you, and I'll make sure you're okay."

Lydia sighed heavily. "I know you mean well, John, but I can't just walk away from this problem."

"I don't see how you can help, Lydia. You can't commit someone to counseling or to an institution when there is no evidence that there's a problem. You know that."

"I do know that, so that's why I've been trying to get to know them so I could guide them."

"That's totally honorable and commendable, my darling, but it is not advisable. Let your good Doctor John counsel you. Come away with me. We'll build yet another house far away from here, so you can forget this problem. We'll adopt a herd of children for you to worry over, and we'll work together to save a small portion of the world."

Lydia moved from the porch rail and paced up and down before coming to stand in front of him. "John, you're making fun of me."

John pulled her into his arms and kissed her. "No, darling, I'm not. I love you for wanting to save these kids, and I love you for loving me. You do, don't you?"

Lydia snuggled against him and let her heart sigh in pleasure. "Yes, I do. That's why I turned to you with this problem, I'm sure."

"I don't know if I can help, but if you want me to, I'll try."

John Worries

John checked the clock again—5:00 a.m., and he couldn't sleep. He threw back the covers, causing Scrap to leap off the bed and scamper down the stairs to his plate in the kitchen.

John stood there, surveying the contents of the refrigerator.

"You're expecting a treat, Scrap? Remember what the vet said about snacks? We need to trim you down."

It was too early for coffee, so he poured a glass of apple juice and went to his office. Scrap followed along and leaped onto the desk.

"What do you think, old boy? Anything we can do to help our fair lady Lydia with her problem kids? Maybe we need to distract her instead. Permanently. How would you feel about sharing our bed with her?"

He scratched the cat's chin and rubbed behind his ears, and Scrap showed his appreciation with a low rumbling purr that made John smile.

While he brushed Scrap, he reviewed what he knew about the Johnson family. They had come here from Atlanta, with the idea of giving their family a fresh start. They'd purchased the old Swanson place and put considerable effort and money into transforming it. They had become active in the community, so it was a sad time when the accident occurred, leaving two teenagers behind, each of them adopted and without any known family. The community had rallied around them, as was their way. While the rest of the world may have decided that government agencies could handle problems such as this, Hollyville took pride in taking care of their own.

A few hours later, John had made progress with paperwork at his desk and was finishing a second cup of coffee when George Randolph paid him a surprise visit.

John motioned George to the extra chair in one corner of the office.

"Care for a cup of coffee, George?"

"I'll pass. Had my quota for the day."

George began. "I could use a little advice about some construction. I've had this acreage for a while now. Truthfully, I've been so concerned about the economy, I was afraid to make a move on anything."

"Right. As you know, I've had more time to work on my own house, due to the lack of construction. It's been a pleasant change, but I'm at the spot where I'd welcome some new business."

George scratched his beard for a moment. "I'm thinking we might see more people staying in the country instead of traveling abroad, so maybe it's a good time to add another cabin."

"Things have changed for travelers, for sure. It's probably a safe bet that you'll have no trouble finding renters. Or were you thinking of selling?"

"No, I want to hold on to the land as long as I can. Why? You got somebody in mind who wants to buy? That lady friend of yours?" George winked.

John paused. "News travels fast around here, I see."

"Well now, you couldn't expect otherwise." George reached to pat John's shoulder. "Truth is we're all mighty pleased for you. Enough time's passed since your wife died, and you're too young to be going it alone. Besides that, Lydia is a real nice person, far as I can tell."

"I'll admit I've been lonely. Physical labor helps, but it's not a permanent answer."

"You thinking of finishing up your house for you and Lydia?"

John lowered his gaze. "We haven't talked about that."

"Well now, sure hope you aren't planning on leaving us."

John shifted in his chair and crossed one leg over the other. "I honestly don't know."

"Spect she'd want to keep on with her college job. That's a pretty good meal ticket, if you know what I mean."

John stood up, walked to his desk, picked up a notebook, and settled into his office chair.

George took the hint. "I guess I was getting a little too personal there, John. Hope you'll excuse me."

John nodded. "Should we get down to business?"

"Sure, but one more thing. You see Jan Johnson around here lately?"

"Not that I remember. Why?"

"Ruth says she's seen her in the woods more than usual. We know she's a hiker and that she's out and about all the time, but Ruth is a little worried. Last time she saw her, the girl was racing through the woods by our place and she dropped to the ground. Ruth thought maybe she was hurt, but it was more like the girl was disturbed. She got up after a bit and started circling round a tree, doing some kind of dance. Not normal, if you know what I mean."

"Really?"

George plunged ahead. "I know Lydia's been concerned about Jan; she talked with us about it. It was that time after the big storm and we brought Lydia down to our house for some breakfast. Seemed like she thought Bryce was treating Jan wrong, from the way she talked. Said she wanted to help them if she could."

John looked down at his notebook.

"Now I'm not one for gossip, and Ruth knows this, but maybe we need to be concerned. We're a community, after all, and we've been watching out for those two ever since the accident."

"It's certainly a concern," John said. "As far as I know, Lydia wants to help Jan and Bryce go to college, which seems like a good idea. Maybe that would take care of whatever troubles the kids are having. Certainly, I have to agree with Lydia that they could benefit from getting an education."

"Well now, just between us, college isn't the answer to everything. They'd just take their troubles with them."

John nodded and waited.

"Girl like Jan needs her father about now, more than ever. Needs some guidance, if you know what I mean."

John looked at George.

"You understand, John. The girl's been trying to be a mother to Bryce, and that's not normal for a young girl. No wonder she's half out of her mind at times. Boy's had a history of troubles before they got here and has a temper to this day."

John continued to nod and to wait.

"Things been brewing all this time. Girl's bound to go off the deep end a bit."

"You've seen other things that worry you, then?" John asked.

"Ruth tells me things. Jan talked with Ruth a lot for a time. Right up until this summer. She'd be out in the woods and would stop by. Ruth would give her tea and cake or cookies, whatever she'd been baking, and it got to be a natural thing for them to visit regularly. Ruth was really into it, kind of being a mother for Jan, I suppose. Eventually, Jan told Ruth about finding the car crashed in the stream over the side of the mountain."

Both men let out a heavy sigh.

"That's an awful burden for a young girl to carry around in her head, John."

"I don't suppose they had counseling, other than the usual help from the school counselor."

"Ruth wanted to help them get counseling, but I was afraid for us to get involved with that, so I kept insisting that she stay out of it. Now I have to wonder if I made a mistake."

"It's a hard call, George. None of us has much experience with this kind of thing."

"According to Ruth, the girl felt guilty about her parents' death."

"Sometimes it's normal for people left behind to feel guilt, survivor guilt I think it's called. That's what they call it in war time."

"Anyway, Jan started showing Ruth some of her sketches, and all of them had borders with some weird kind of pattern, some kind of figures, symbols maybe. Ruth said it looked sinister, but I don't know. Might have been just a design. Ruth can get a little carried away at times."

John remembered Lydia's description of the border, remembered that it resembled the message in the box and the carving on the tree.

"Then there was the time when Jan had a little breakdown. We were really worried about that, but we decided not to tell anybody about it. There wasn't much we could do."

"A breakdown? What do you mean?"

"The girl was sobbing and carrying on, said she didn't care if she lived, felt trapped by Bryce. Said everybody loves Bryce's artwork. Mentioned Lydia and how taken she is with the boxes. Said she knows her art is nothing, that she'll never be able to be as good as he is. Went on and on about being left behind by her parents, with no future, and said she had to find a way to get out of here."

"Do you think she's suicidal?"

"Maybe. I don't know anything about things like that. Maybe it was just things pressing at her more than usual. Ruth said she comforted her as best she could, but she worried even more after that, 'cause Jan stopped talking about anything personal, and then she stopped coming by. The other day was the first she's been around in weeks. And as I told you, she sure wasn't acting normal that day. Do you think we need to do something, John?"

"I really don't know."

"Maybe it's best to let it alone for now."

"Maybe so. Let's get back to your construction plans."

The men continued their discussion of plans for an additional rental cottage that John would build.

Trouble in the Woods

Lydia awoke with a flood of images and feelings for John flowing around and through her. She had half a mind to drive to his house again this morning—right now—catch him before he started work on the house. She laughed at herself. *You're behaving like a teenager.*

She did a few yoga stretches, opened the blinds, saw the blanket of early morning fog, and headed for the shower.

Maybe later today I'll drive over.

Confident that he was just as eager as she was, she would savor these moments. Soon enough, they would make decisions about their future.

She continued to postpone the discussion of where they might live and whether she would keep her teaching job. She had to admit that John's idea of moving to a new place and starting fresh had lots of appeal, if he had meant it. Maybe he was just making the offer to be romantic.

She hoped they could reach an agreeable compromise. *But what can you expect? This is the way it has to be for people our age. No easy answers.* She frowned. *Stop this. You are lucky beyond lucky. Revel in it.*

After breakfast, Lydia still felt restless, so she decided to go for a walk. It was one of those mornings that made her want to soak up the beauty of the area. She took a moderate pace and let her thoughts roll.

Was nature producing her extra sensitive longings? She had always been responsive to the miracles of wildlife, something she held in common with Jan. She understood perfectly Jan's need to commune with all that she found in these woods. She just didn't understand if something abnormal beckoned Jan to shelter herself here.

Her determination to help Jan and Bryce kept her mind in a muddle. She had not yet faced her feelings about Jan and Bryce; she refused to see that her preoccupation with their relationship was a substitution for solving her own problems. Neither Charles nor John had convinced her that she was meddling in dangerous territory.

Ten minutes into her walk and only a short distance from the road leading to Jan and Bryce's house, Lydia thought she smelled smoke. She stood still and took in a deep breath. An acrid smell rode the otherwise fresh air. Maybe it was just a trash fire. Sometimes household trash was burned in a container; often an empty oil drum was used in rural areas when there was no pickup service. George Randolph, fortunately for her, came for her trash at the end of each week, but she didn't know if he burned it or hauled it someplace, maybe to a landfill.

She sniffed again, and her eyes traveled upward, where she thought she saw haze, but more likely it was the last of the early morning fog.

She walked on, telling herself it was nothing.

But the smoke brought bad memories crashing into her mind. She had been so young, not yet in school. The entire scene flashed back to her.

She was asleep when her father grabbed her from her bed. He was coughing and choking from the smoke, but he didn't let go of her. She remembered her own coughing and feeling stricken with fear as he carried her to the window. Holding her tight against his chest, he had climbed out of the window onto the porch roof.

Below people were yelling, "The fire truck is coming. Don't jump. You'll get hurt. Wait."

Even now she could hear the fire truck's alarm screaming. And then the truck was on their street, pulling alongside their yard, and men in their firemen's gear jumped to the ground and began their work. A ladder was placed at the edge of the roof, and in a few minutes, someone else was holding her and handing her down to someone below. Her mother.

"Don't cry," she told me. "You're safe now."

"Is everyone out?" one of the men asked, and our neighbor Mr. Hopson from across the street stepped forward to answer the questions.

A crowd formed in the shadows and across the street. A low murmur of voices rose in the night air. She and her mother sat in a lawn chair someone had put at the edge of their yard. Her mother held her close while her father got water for them, and someone gave them a blanket.

Nightmares about that fire plagued her for years afterward.

She knew the power of fire, the wretchedness it could leave behind.

She sniffed again. What if it were a forest fire? If so, she needed to think about retreating. A chill ran down her spine. Maybe she should go back to the cabin now. Get in her car and go for help.

But here she was at the Johnson's lane. Better to check with them, she decided. That was closer, and they may have already called the fire department.

The smoke was harsh, catching in her nostrils, reminding her again of her childhood experience, adding its ominous feeling.

She ran down their driveway. Now she could see black smoke spiraling from the back of the Johnson's house. She didn't remember seeing a trash burning place there. What if the house was on fire or the studio? She ran faster and screamed, "Bryce! Jan!"

If only she had driven, she would have a fast way to get help. Maybe her cell phone would work. She stopped, pulled it from her pocket, and dialed 911, but the signal was breaking up. No time to fuss with that now. The Johnsons would have a landline, surely. She ran on toward their house.

A stream of questions flooded her mind. Where was the fire station?

She didn't remember seeing one in Hollyville, but surely there must be one for the area if not for Hollyville alone. How long would it take firemen to get here? If this fire got out of control, it could be a major disaster. Property and even the entire forest could go up in flames. There had to be a way to get help. To notify people. To get everyone to safety.

Almost at the house, she saw a figure dashing into the woods. Was it Jan or Bryce?

She yelled again. "Jan, Bryce. Help."

She ran to the back of the house and saw the smoke coming from the studio.

When she pulled open the door, a wall of smoke overpowered her. She had to turn away. She had no breath. Her eyes burned and her throat felt constricted. She couldn't speak. Instinctively, she pulled her shirt over her nose and mouth for protection from the smoke.

She ran to the house to get to a phone. The door was open, and as she pushed inside, she let her gaze take in the scene. The hallway opened into a formal living room on one side and an office on the other. A phone rested at the edge of the large desk in the office.

Just as she reached for the phone, she saw Bryce slumped in a heap on the floor on the other side of the desk.

"Oh no, Bryce! What happened?

He didn't answer.

Lydia picked up the phone, dialed 911, and gave the pertinent information about location. "We need an ambulance too," she added.

Next, she called George Randolph to report the fire.

Ruth answered.

"Oh good Lord. What will we do? George isn't here right now. He's gone to Hollyville on an errand. I'll call him on his cell phone, but it's not very reliable."

"I've called 911. How long will it take for help to get here?"

"Did you try the fire extinguisher?"

"No, but I think it may be too late."

"Hollyville has a good station, but it takes a while for the volunteers to get there. Let's hope it isn't too late. What about Jan and Bryce?"

"Bryce is here, but I think I saw Jan leaving. She may have been going for help."

"She may be coming here. I'll watch for her, and you see if you can use the fire extinguisher. There'll be one in the kitchen and another one in the garage. Be careful."

Lydia hung up and returned to Bryce. It took all her effort to roll him over onto his back. She checked for pulse and found one. "Bryce, wake up." She slapped his check to try to rouse him, but he didn't respond.

She ran down the hall to the kitchen, grabbed a towel and ran water over it, and carried it back to Bryce. She rubbed vigorously at his face with the towel.

Bryce let out a moan.

"Bryce, what happened?"

He pushed up on one elbow. "I don't know. I passed out, I guess."

"Bryce, you know about the fire?"

"Yeah, but I didn't have anything to stop it. I tried to save some of my boxes and carvings, but the smoke got me. Where's Jan?"

"I think I saw her running into the woods, maybe to go for help."

"Right. She told me to call 911."

"And you just passed out?"

"I had an asthma attack, and I got in here and got my inhaler, but I still passed out. I do that sometimes."

"Can you stand up? Help me get the fire extinguishers and maybe the garden hose going."

BLOCKED

Bryce struggled to his feet and started to the kitchen for the fire extinguisher while Lydia went to the yard to find the garden hose.

Lydia had stretched the hose as far as it would go and was directing the water on the studio when John drove into the parking area.

"Oh my God, Lydia, are you all right?"

Complications

Lydia felt the tension in her body easing as soon as John arrived. He would be able to help. Already he had a fire extinguisher from his truck and was moving toward the studio with it.

"Direct the water on the back side of the studio," he told Lydia. "That'll keep the fire from spreading."

"Bryce, over here, with that extinguisher."

It didn't seem possible, but within minutes, the fire was almost under control.

John told Lydia, "I'll take over here with the hose. You tend to Bryce. He's having trouble breathing. Probably inhaled some of the smoke. Check him for burns."

Lydia took Bryce inside the house and helped him get situated on the couch in the office. She positioned pillows to elevate his head.

"Where is your inhaler, Bryce?"

He struggled to pull it from his pocket, and Lydia lifted his head while he sprayed and inhaled.

"I sent for an ambulance. We'll get you to the hospital so you can have oxygen and a good checking."

Bryce started to get up but then fell back into the stack of pillows.

"I'll be all right." He gasped and coughed. "I don't want to go to the hospital."

"We'll see. Right now, I want you to rest."

She pulled a chair near the couch so she could monitor Bryce's breathing.

He appeared to be breathing easier.

"I'll be right back to check on you."

She went to find John.

"Should I cancel the ambulance and the fire department? I don't think we need them now. We can take Bryce to the hospital ourselves."

"I already called."

"Your cell phone worked? I couldn't get through on mine earlier."

"Right. Reception is spotty out here. You think Bryce needs to go to the hospital?"

"I'd feel better if we took him."

"Maybe let him rest for a while. I can't leave this yet. You never know when the fire might spring up again. It's still too dangerous to go inside, but later I'll go in and check everything."

Lydia hugged John. "Please don't take any chances."

"You're shivering."

"I was frightened out of my mind. I could see the entire forest go up in flames."

"It could have happened."

"I'm so glad you came along when you did." Lydia was still one calm debate away from convincing Bryce to go to the hospital.

"No, you don't understand. I need to be here."

"John is taking care of things. He'll make sure the fire doesn't erupt again."

"It's not that. I need to be here when Jan comes back."

"But we don't know when she'll return, and right now, the most important thing is to make sure you are okay."

"I'm fine."

Bryce began coughing and wheezing again.

"That's it. We're going."

Lydia helped him get up and put her arm around him for support. "Lean on me."

She walked Bryce outside and got him into John's truck. She called over her shoulder to John, "May I have your keys?"

John brought the keys to her. "Call me. Okay?" He brushed her cheek with a quick kiss before returning to his vigil.

<hr />

Bryce was exhausted. He slumped back against the seat and closed his eyes.

Within twenty minutes, they were at the local emergency care facility where Lydia explained the situation, registered Bryce, and saw that he was admitted.

"There's no need for you to stay, Ms. Drexel. Give us your phone number, and we'll call you when we have a report. We'll monitor him throughout the night, and if everything checks out well, he could probably go home sometime tomorrow or the next day. We'll need a doctor's clearance on that though."

Lydia handed the nurse her business card.

"Thank you."

Back at the fire scene, Lydia found John assessing the exterior of the studio.

"How bad is it?"

"I checked inside for hot spots, and things seem to be okay as far as I can tell. There's less damage than I expected. Mostly smoke and some water damage. It's fixable."

"But the artwork?"

"I don't know."

"Is it okay for me to go in?"

"We'll go together. Just give me a few more minutes here. I want to be doubly sure that everything out here is okay. One hot coal and one bit of wind, and we could have a whole new story."

The interior walls were charred at the front end of the studio, and some of the windows were broken. Puddles of water stood on the floor near the broken windows.

"I've got some plywood in the truck. I'll use it to cover the windows until we can replace the glass."

"Oh John, you are so generous."

"Ah, more points for me." He laughed.

"You know how much I love your laugh?"

"Enough to marry me?"

"Almost."

"Uh, not the answer I was looking for."

"And not the best moment to ask?"

John embraced Lydia and whispered in her ear, "But I'll keep on asking."

"Please do."

John gave her a tender kiss and suggested that they get busy cleaning up the place.

They worked well together, taking only a few breaks.

After a couple of hours, the worst of the mess was gone. John used a Shop-Vac he'd found in the storage area while Lydia wiped down the workbenches and the exposed carvings and boxes.

"Where do you think the fire started?" she asked.

"Usually, it's a faulty electrical connection."

John began to search the building, checking the outlets, examining the areas where the most damage occurred.

"I'm not officially qualified to judge, but I think something in this trash bin near the door could have been the cause. Maybe old rags ignited somehow. See how much more affected the area is right here, especially the ceiling?"

"But surely the trash wouldn't just automatically ignite."

"No, something was probably dropped there carelessly. Is either of them a smoker?"

"I don't know, but I doubt it."

"Maybe a partially spent match?"

"Oh, my goodness. It just occurred to me that we should have left everything alone. How will they collect from their insurance?"

"I doubt that a fire on such a small scale would yield that much from their insurance."

"Oh, right. I don't know much about that end of things. I only vaguely remember my parents talking about insurance for our house fire."

John looked at her with surprise. "You were in a house fire?"

"Yes, it was terrifying. I had nightmares for years, and it all came back with this fire."

"My poor darling." John held her tenderly.

After a moment, Lydia pulled away reluctantly. "I'll tell you about it later. We'd better finish this."

"Right."

"Thank goodness Jan and Bryce were good about storing their finished work. Even the boxes and carvings that were left out will be okay. Only the drawings Jan left on top of the drawing board are damaged."

Lydia grabbed John's arm. "I just thought of something. Maybe we destroyed the clues."

"Clues? Have you suddenly shifted into detective-mode?"

"Maybe. Jan should have returned by now."

"Are you sure she hasn't? Maybe she's inside."

"I don't think so. Wouldn't she come in here immediately?"

"Probably, so where is she?"

Lydia headed toward the door. "We have to see if we can find her."

John reached for Lydia's hand. "Whoa, there. That's not our concern, darling."

"It's *my* concern. I won't be able to sleep tonight if I don't know where she is. She would be terribly upset over the fire and the loss of the art, wouldn't she? And when she's upset, she always goes into the woods."

"So you think she's been wandering around in the woods all this time? Surely not. Didn't you say you thought she'd gone to get help? Maybe she went to see the Randolphs."

"Maybe. But it's possible that she's out there in the woods."

"Let's be sensible, Lyd. If she's missing in the morning, we'll get some help."

Lydia Searches for Jan

By the time Lydia got home, she was more exhausted than she had ever been. However, restful sleep eluded her. She spent hours attempting to read, but her concentration was shot.

At 6:00 a.m., she kicked off her tangled bed covers and went to the kitchen to put on a pot of coffee. As she reached for a mug, she turned on the radio.

"In local news, Fire Chief Gordon Henry said someone placed a false call for service at 11:38 a.m. yesterday. According to Henry, the caller reported a fire at the old Swanson place on Randolph Mountain, but less than an hour later, before volunteers could get to the station, the request was cancelled. No further details are available at this time."

Lydia marveled at this unusual community. Who would expect to hear such a report on the radio? Randolph Mountain? Was that what the locals called it? Strange, the way local lore could spring up quite by chance, at least to a newcomer.

After breakfast, she called the Randolphs to see if they knew anything about Jan, but there was no answer. She decided not to leave a message. It was senseless to cause unnecessary alarm.

She pondered whether she should go to the house to see if Jan had returned during the night. While it was the logical thing to do, it was not what she wanted to do. It would be better if she could wipe away her memories of fires of any kind, not to mention her concerns over Jan, but she told herself to put things in perspective.

BLOCKED

There was no better option, so she took some care with dressing, knowing that her second stop would be the local police station if she failed to find Jan at home.

At the Johnsons', Lydia knocked at the front door and waited. No response. She knew Jan might not answer, so she turned the knob. The door was unlocked.

"Jan, are you here?" There was no answer.

After several calls for Jan, she gave up. But why was the door open? She was sure that she had locked it before she left yesterday. Was Jan inside hiding?

Going against her instincts, she went inside and called again, but there was still no answer. She went to the back of the house to Jan's bedroom, but she was not there, and she stood at the foot of the stairs, calling again.

She hesitated before going upstairs to check the second floor. She tried to resist the feel that she was "breaking and entering," invading someone's personal space without permission, looking for evidence, but surely it was the only sensible action. She found nothing, set the lock on the door before leaving, thinking, *should I have been wearing gloves*? She chuckled at herself.

Outside, she walked around the house, just to check things, not knowing what to look for, just checking.

At the studio, she saw that John had returned, as promised, and tacked plywood over the broken windows. Inside, things looked the same. No longer an inviting place, the studio was dark and dingy. The acrid odor from the fire lingered. Despite their efforts to put the place in order, it would not be a welcoming sight for either Jan or Bryce. She wondered if Jan had returned and then left again. That could account for the door being unlocked.

With no time to linger, Lydia decided she should get some help finding

Jan.

As she drove toward the village, she wondered if the local authorities would be cooperative. Sensing that a bad impression could hamper the results, that the police might question her right to be involved, she tried to prepare herself.

"I have every right to take action. It's the responsible thing to do."

At the municipal building, Lydia parked in the rear, and inside, she found a directory posted in the entrance. Obviously, Hollyville officials had planned well. They had combined most of the city offices in this one building. A receptionist welcomed her and directed her to the appropriate office.

Officer Degan told Lydia to take a seat.

"What can I do for you?"

Lydia took a deep breath. Officer Degan looked like he had been here at least as long as the building and perhaps longer. She hoped he would be sympathetic, but there was no way of knowing. She had learned that young people and seniors could be equally limited in their perspectives. Or equally open, she reminded herself.

"I need help finding a young woman who's missing. Jan Johnson. She and her brother Bryce live on the old Swanson place." Lydia thought how strange it was that she had fallen into the local idiom so quickly.

"Oh yeah, the old Swanson place. The young kids whose parents died in a car crash a few years back."

She watched as he leaned back in the swivel chair and ran his hand through his thinning grey hair. And was that an affectionate pat he was giving his bald spot? If so, it made her want to smile.

Although she hoped for a positive reception, she had no idea what he was thinking. Her intuition told her to be cautious.

"This have anything to do with that erroneous call for help yesterday?"

She noted the officer's tone of voice. She didn't like the extra emphasis he placed on the word *erroneous*, but she decided to let it pass, to keep a positive approach.

"Actually, it does."

Lydia explained how she had discovered the fire, and how with Bryce and John's help, they had been able to get the small fire under control."

"And Miss Johnson was not there at the time?"

Lydia wondered if she should report she had seen Jan leaving the scene. She admitted to herself that she had no proof it was Jan leaving, and she hadn't yet decided if Jan had something to do with the fire.

"No, she wasn't."

"What time did you arrive at the house, Ms. Drexel?"

Lydia realized she had only an estimated time. Automatically, she looked at her watch, as if it would tell her. "It was late morning, around eleven o'clock, I think."

"I see."

The officer shuffled through a stack of papers, found and opened a file folder.

"The 911 call came in at 11:38." He glanced up and then back at the folder, as if there were some important and unusual information there.

Lydia felt the officer's questioning gaze. After a moment of silence, she cleared her throat and continued.

"I just thought it was unusual for Jan not to be there yesterday, not to return during the afternoon when we were cleaning things up, and not to be there this morning, so I wanted to see if there were some way to get help finding her."

Officer Degan shifted in his chair, as if his hip pained him.

"So, you're telling me you cleaned up things at the fire. Exactly what did that involve, Ms. Drexel?"

Lydia had a small sensation of fear. Had they been wrong? Would she be accused of tampering with evidence?

"We wanted to see if the artwork was damaged, but only some of Jan's drawings were spoiled from the water that came inside. Most everything was stored in containers."

Lydia went on, telling the officer about vacuuming up the water, wiping the workbenches, and John's efforts to cover the broken windows.

"I suspect John Crawford, being a builder, could determine something about how the fire started, but normally, most folks would leave that work for the fire chief and his people to make those decisions."

There was a silence.

Lydia wanted to defend herself, but she also believed that she should not have to. She looked down at her lap for a time before she returned her gaze to Officer Degan.

"Just how do you happen to know the Johnsons?"

Lydia explained how she had become acquainted with Jan and Bryce Johnson, telling about their interest in art, but she had a feeling Officer Degan questioned her right to be there. Was this more of the small, closed community approach she was feeling, or was it a typical kind of questioning that any police department would use? She'd had almost no experience with this kind of thing, so perhaps that colored her perceptions.

"Terrible tragedy those two young people experienced, losing their parents like that, but they seem to have come through it with flying colors."

Was this his way of eliciting information, or was it simply a positive evaluation of the situation? Should she tell him her concerns? She sensed that he would not approve.

"The community, I understand, has gathered around them to give support."

She waited for Officer Degan to respond, but he continued to study the folder in front of him.

"Is there something more that I need to do, Officer Degan?"

"More to do?" Again he shifted his weight in the chair.

"I mean, will there be a search?"

The officer smiled in what Lydia perceived to be a condescending way. Then he hoisted himself from the chair and extended his hand. Lydia rose and accepted the hand.

"Pleasure to meet you, Ms. Drexel. We'll tend to your report in due time."

"In due time?"

"Yes, ma'am, in due time."

Lydia filled out the necessary forms and left, feeling that the officer was probably scribbling notes that were not in her favor. She wished she had not gone to anyone official but had used the more common methods of the community. Her next stop would be the Randolphs' house.

A Surprise Encounter

Lydia rubbed her brow to ease the nagging headache. She checked her handbag and the glove compartment but found no aspirin. Her pills were back at her cabin.

Damn it, Lydia, why aren't you better organized?

Should she drive to the cabin before going to the Randolphs'? This headache would only get worse without medication. She took some deep breaths and coaxed her shoulders to drop into relaxation.

You're wanting things to be easy, to be wrapped up and out of the way, but that's not likely to happen. So just hang on.

For a few seconds, she heard Charles warning her to stop. Back off. Let it go. She thought briefly about calling him. Even though he admonished her from time to time, he always listened attentively, always gave comfort.

What she really wanted right now was to see John. She had been bowled over by the way he had helped her, giving directions to her and Bryce, remaining calm and efficient until the fire in the studio was under control. She knew more than ever that she wanted John to be a part of her life.

She could drive to his place right now, but that wouldn't take away the problem with Jan. She couldn't get rid of the feeling that Jan was in trouble, that she had to find her.

She had little hope Officer Degan would take action, at least not any time soon. No doubt he'd be too busy checking his bald spot.

Once again, she was on her own.

BLOCKED

When Lydia pulled into the Randolphs' driveway, she saw that George Randolph's truck was not there. Her head throbbed. She had hoped he would help her find Jan.

For some reason she never considered, Lydia bypassed the front door and went straight to the side entrance. She jiggled the doorknob instead of knocking.

The door opened onto a landing. A short flight of stairs led up to the kitchen and the remaining stairs went down into what appeared to be a storage area or perhaps a workshop. Without lighting, it was difficult to tell.

She called, "Hello? Anyone home?"

Scraping sounds on the floor above puzzled her. It sounded like a dog pushing its bowl around on the floor, but she was sure the Randolphs had no pets. Maybe Ruth just hadn't heard her.

"Ruth? Hello, it's Lydia Drexel."

What was that muffled sound? A strangled voice? Ruth must be ill. *Oh good God, she's had a stroke.*

Fear gripped Lydia.

She ran up the short flight of stairs. What she saw boggled her brain. Shock ran through her body. She could not have imagined such a scene.

Blood dripped from Jan's arms and legs where she had slashed herself with a knife she held in her trembling right hand. The wounds seemed to form some kind of pattern. The note in the box and symbols carved into the tree flashed into Lydia's mind.

Ruth was tied to a kitchen chair with twine. Her mouth was gagged with a towel, and blood was oozing from the cuts on her biceps.

Lydia felt faint when she saw the look of terror in Ruth's eyes. Was Jan trying to kill Ruth?

"Oh dear God, what's going on? What have you done?"

"Stop. Don't come near me," Jan said. Her voice was cold and controlling, as she thrust the bloody knife toward Lydia.

Lydia's mind raced. *It's as if she can't stop herself.*

What could she say to make Jan relax? How could she get Jan to drop the knife? She knew she needed help. *You were stupid to come here alone.*

Afraid to make any sudden movements, she turned slightly to her right, away from Jan, and slipped her hand into her pocket for her cell phone. She waited for the right moment. Jan was too volatile. Anything could happen. Ruth strained against the ropes and tried to tilt the chair. Obviously, she was losing strength.

"Ruth, stay quiet," Lydia warned. "Save your strength." Lydia turned to Jan. "Please, Jan, you have to listen to me."

Jan mocked, "I *have* to listen to you? You don't want me. You only want Bryce. He's the talented one. No one wants to listen to me."

"Oh Jan, dear, no. No. You have a future too. Your talent matters just as much, but you've got to stop this. Trust me, please. You've got to give yourself a chance."

Jan began to sob.

"A chance? What kind of chance do I have? My future died with my parents in a fire the night of the crash."

"Jan, it's not too late." Lydia extended her hand. "Please, just give me the knife."

"No! Stay back. Stupid bitch." Jan spread her feet apart in a defensive stance and thrust the knife toward Lydia. "I have to put these symbols everywhere. It's the only way to purify us."

Lydia remembered the research Charles had sent her. Native American folklore cited symbols that could heal. *But heal what? The symbol for fire represented either purification of land or something about renewing life. Jan must have read about it too.*

Lydia knew she had to distract Jan somehow. Put the attention on someone else.

"Jan, we have to take Ruth to the hospital. She's getting weaker by the minute. Let me call for an ambulance."

Lydia pulled her cell phone from her pocket.

"Drop it!" Jan darted toward Lydia and knocked the cell phone from her hand, causing Lydia to jump back. She felt a sharp pain followed by a dull warmness. A few seconds passed before she realized she had bumped into the sharp corner of the island in the middle of the kitchen.

Lydia took a deep breath and tried to stand up straight.

"Jan, dear, please listen. You don't want Ruth to be in pain. She might even die. Please help me take her to the doctor."

Jan sank back and turned to look at Ruth. For a moment Lydia sensed her plan was working. She took advantage of the moment to step closer to Jan and Ruth, but Jan whirled around and struck a glancing blow to Lydia's upper arm.

Lydia gasped and instinctively grabbed at her arm. *Concentrate. Don't panic. Appeal to Jan.*

"Jan, listen to me, please, before you kill one of us and ruin any chance you still have. This is not the message behind your symbol. Think of what you're doing. The symbol is about healing."

"Stay back. I know what I'm doing. The symbol will save us. Give me your arm, Lydia, so I can save you too."

Lydia marveled at the way the human mind could become so twisted and tormented.

"Jan, I know you don't want to hurt Ruth after all she's done for you, all she's meant to you. We have to get help immediately. Look at her."

"I know what I'm doing. I'm not falling for that trick again."

Jan pointed the knife toward Lydia. "Get back."

Lydia obeyed.

Jan turned toward Ruth and held the knife at her throat. Ruth moaned and struggled.

"Do what I tell you, or else," Jan shouted at Lydia.

Lydia tried not to think of the blood on her arm or what might happen to Ruth, as she became keenly aware of the sweat trickling down her back.

Jan gestured toward the second chair at the nearby table. "Get that chair. Scoot it over here beside Ruth."

Lydia paused, trying to decide if it was worth it to lunge for the knife. Could she get into the right position? Was she strong enough to pull Jan's arm behind her back, in a hold that would force her to drop the knife?

"Get the chair," Jan screamed. "Now!"

Lydia moved toward the chair, her mind whirling. She thought of using the chair as a weapon. If she could move quickly enough and get enough force behind it, she could knock Jan to the floor.

At that moment, Lydia heard a motor. It sounded like John's truck. He would see her car in the driveway. She hoped it would be a clue that she was in trouble. If only she could warn him.

Lydia saw Jan cock her head toward the sound of the motor. She knew Jan might recognize it as John's truck because of the distinct sound of its diesel engine. Would this change her plans? With a little luck, Jan would return to her usual pattern of behavior and run to her haven, the forest. She could just as easily react like a caged animal. From the look in Jan's eyes, that was exactly what Lydia expected.

Lydia watched for a chance to take Jan by surprise.

Jan hissed, "Not a sound, or I'll use this. Stay back, Lydia. I mean it." She placed the knife tip closer to Ruth's throat.

Lydia saw the panic in Ruth's eyes, felt Ruth recoil both emotionally and physically, and heard the pleading in her strangled voice.

The truck door slammed, and within seconds, they heard knocking on the door.

"Hello."

Ruth struggled, but Lydia motioned for her to remain quiet.

"Ruth? It's John Crawford."

Lydia saw Jan shiver.

For a moment, the hand holding the knife relaxed enough for Lydia to take a chance. She raised the chair at chest height and ran at Jan. The chair legs struck her in the chest, causing Jan to drop the knife and fall backward on the floor.

John rushed in just as Jan hit the floor. "Oh my God, Lydia, what's going on? Are you all right? Ruth, who did this to you?"

Jan, stunned by Lydia's attack, remained on the floor, whimpering.

Lydia stood up. Her voice trembled. "Thank God you're here."

Lydia removed the gag from Ruth's mouth while John cut the ties around her wrists with his pocketknife. John stopped to pull a bandana from his pocket and motioned toward the corner. "Here, Lydia. Get that knife."

Lydia stooped to pick up the knife that lay a few feet away from Jan.

In a split second, Jan let out a blood-curdling scream and grabbed Lydia around the ankles, slamming her to the floor, away from the knife.

John turned from Ruth in time to grab Jan by the hair and then her arms. He pushed her into the empty chair. "Now sit there while I get this mess straightened out."

Lydia noted the dominating control in John's voice and doubted anyone would think of refusing his command—especially a sick child.

Jan appeared to be calm and docile—as she sat slumped in the chair.

While Lydia examined Ruth's superficial wounds, she tried to reassure her. "I'm so sorry this happened to you. We'll get you to a doctor. Everything will be all right."

Ruth was shaking and sobbing. "George. I want George. Get George."

"She's in shock. I'll find a blanket."

Lydia returned with a blanket for Ruth.

"Let's take her to the hospital."

"What about Jan?" John asked.

"We can't leave her here."

"You're right. We'll take her with us. She needs medical attention too," John said.

Lydia knelt beside Jan. "Come on, Jan, let's go."

Jan stood up slowly, wobbly and depleted, like a limp doll. She leaned into Lydia and cried softly while Lydia held her.

"You're going to be okay, Jan. We'll take care of you."

Jan Tells her Story

They sat in the waiting room in the hospital's psychiatric wing.

Someone had attempted to bring cheerfulness to the room with the sunshine-yellow walls, framed prints depicting seascapes, comfortable chairs, and sofa. Stacks of current magazines on the coffee table presented a distraction, and the friendly receptionist had offered a beverage while they waited.

Lydia was glad they had the room to themselves. Perhaps she could help Jan stay calm.

Slumped against Lydia on the couch, Jan murmured quietly.

"I didn't mean it. I didn't mean it."

Lydia held her hand and spoke softly. "It's okay. Everything will be fine. You're safe now."

"I didn't mean it. I don't know what happens. It's like I'm not really there. Someone else is doing all those things."

Lydia waited for Jan to go on.

"I get so mixed up about things."

Lydia cautioned herself. *Go easy. Don't force anything. Be still. Wait.*

"I want to be good. I really, really want to be good."

"Yes, I know. I understand." Lydia paused. *What's she thinking, feeling? Let her take the lead. Be patient. Calm. Loving. Poor, poor dear. A bundle of confusion.*

"After we moved here, for a while, things were fine. Then Bryce started talking about who his real parents might be, what might have happened to them, and stuff like that. I was pretty sure he was searching on the computer. It was making me scared. I thought he might go with his parents if he found them and leave me. I knew they wouldn't take both of us."

"That had to be a difficult time for both of you. You probably wanted to know about your parents too."

Lydia watched Jan shred a tissue into strips and then twist all of it into a ball. She rolled the ball around and around in the palm of her hand.

"I wanted to be the good big sister, but it was so hard."

"I know what you mean. I felt the same way about being the big sister in my family."

Jan turned slightly and looked into Lydia's face. She drew a long breath before nestling against Lydia again.

"Sometimes I just wanted things to be right for me. Bryce, Bryce, Bryce. Everything was always for Bryce. What about me?"

Lydia sensed Jan's change in mood and anticipated a change in her behavior.

"You thought they loved him more."

Jan sat up and looked at Lydia.

"Oh yeah. I *knew* they loved him more."

Lydia saw the anger in Jan's eyes. For a moment, Lydia thought Jan would bolt from the room. But just as suddenly, the anger melted away, and Jan sank back into the sofa.

The receptionist looked up from her desk and slid open the glass window. She made eye contact with Lydia. Lydia responded with a smile.

The window remained open.

Jan sat slumped and silent, her head bowed forward, her knees pulled against her chest.

"Fire. It's good. It cleanses and takes away the bad. It restores life. Brings hope. I wanted all of us to start over. To be free and happy again.

I had to find a way to help us."

"But fire can destroy too."

"It wasn't supposed to destroy. I read about it, how the Native Americans used it in their rituals, how it helped them."

Lydia waited for Jan to continue.

"I wasn't supposed to hear them. They thought I was asleep, but I'd gotten up to go to the bathroom, and I stood by their door. It was open, and I could hear them talking. That's when I found out."

"Yes?"

"About my real parents, that it was my mother, not Bryce's who was raped by a criminal."

"But, Jan, dear, are you sure you heard right? You might have misunderstood."

Lydia sensed the rigidity radiating from Jan.

"No. I know. I know what happened."

Lydia saw the intensity and heard the confidence in Jan's voice, as if no one could ever question her on this fact.

"My mother went insane. She wanted to keep me, but they wouldn't let her."

Jan rocked gently forward and back. Lydia placed a hand on her back and stroked gently in a circular motion, trying to calm the girl.

"They locked her up. But she tricked them. She fooled them into making them think she was well so she could get out of there. She wouldn't let them take her away a second time. She committed suicide."

"Oh, my dear," Lydia began.

Jan jerked away when Lydia offered a hug.

"Let me finish. You have to understand. You have to know what happened."

"I'm listening, Jan."

"She went into the woods so she could be alone, so she could find peace. And I kept thinking all along I could find peace there, too. I've tried so hard. I carved the symbols in the tree so the message of healing could spread everywhere."

Lydia wondered if Jan was capable of telling the real story. Her reading about mental illness and her own experience with her sister made her aware that the facts were likely to be distorted, that Jan's emotional state would affect her perception of reality. But she continued to listen for bits of the truth, hints of what Jan knew and what she perceived. It was possible that she would reveal some helpful information about what had motivated her actions.

"She didn't want them to know the truth. She had to protect everyone, so she had to keep the secret."

"The secret?"

"Yes, that fire can save the world, can save all of us."

"So, you set the studio on fire?"

"Both times."

"Both times?"

"The first time was just a little one, a symbolic one, to give me courage for a bigger one. It got a little bigger than I planned, and Bryce had to help me put it out."

"Where was the fire?"

"In a big ceramic bowl in the studio. I thought it was dead, but somehow the papers nearby caught on fire, and I was slapping at it with a shirt when Bryce came in, got the fire extinguisher, and put it out."

"That was the night of the car accident, wasn't it?"

Jan gave Lydia a puzzled look. "How did you know that?"

For a moment, Lydia didn't know what to say. She had to be careful. "Something Bryce said."

"What? What did Bryce say?"

Lydia stalled for time.

"Oh, it's nothing. I can't remember exactly."

Jan continued to look baffled until Lydia changed the subject.

"Weren't you afraid of destroying the artwork?"

"No. I was guided by the voices that told me to do it."

"Do you still hear the voices?"

"No, not right now."

"And the voices told you to hurt Ruth?"

Jan gave Lydia a disturbed look. "I didn't hurt Ruth."

"Jan, you gagged her, tired her up, and made cuts in her arms with a knife."

"I was saving her with the fire symbols. Just like the voices told me."

Jan stood up. "Where is she? I have to go to her."

At that moment, the receptionist said, "Ms. Johnson, the doctor will see you now."

Lydia stood with Jan, her arm around Jan's shoulders.

"Ms. Drexel, will you wait here, please?"

Jan turned to Lydia. The look of uncertainty in Jan's eyes drew Lydia back in time. It was if her own sister stood before her, wanting reassurance that help awaited her on the other side of the door.

"It's all right, Jan. I'll be here when you're through. I promise."

Lydia longed to go with Jan, to offer support, and to learn what the doctor would say, but she had known the doctor would want to see Jan alone. She returned to her place on the couch to wait. It was important for Jan to know she had waited for her, that she had not abandoned her. She hoped she would be permitted to see Jan again, but she understood the typical hospital procedures.

She knew it was more than likely that Jan would be admitted for observation. The doctor would see Jan shifting in and out of reality. With medication, it would be possible for Jan to become stable, at least if she could be supervised. But so many patients failed to take their meds. They convinced themselves when they began to feel better that they no longer needed the pills. Or, as it had been in her sister's case, they despaired over the side effects, believing they had been poisoned by the meds.

Lydia hadn't noticed many signs of paranoia in Jan's behavior, so perhaps it would be avoided. What a blessing that would be. But she had mentioned voices, and she knew that was a bad sign.

For a few moments, Lydia thought again about her sister's illness. The shadow of that time when none of the family or the doctors had been able to give lasting help hung over her.

But medications had improved, and therapy could bring relief.

Lydia had hope for Jan.

George Talks with Dr. Davis

George drove as fast as he could over the back roads and faster when he reached the main road. Ruth's wounds didn't seem to be life threatening, but her panic was palpable. Ruth clutched the wool blanket tightly around her shoulders and continued to shiver.

"Ruth, honey, you're going to be fine. I called Dr. Davis. He's expecting us."

Ruth moaned softly and moved her head from side to side. "I can't understand, George."

He could barely hear her. "What, honey? I didn't get that." He leaned toward her.

"Jan. What went wrong, George?"

"I don't know. Some kind of breakdown. John and Lydia are taking care of her. She'll be okay."

"I couldn't get her to listen to me."

"Ruth, we're not going to think about any of that right now. Just try to rest, sweetheart. We'll be there soon."

॰॰॰

In the examination room, Dr. Davis took his time checking Ruth, probing gently, asking her what hurt, speaking in a soothing voice. When he was satisfied with his exam, he instructed the nurse to cleanse and dress the wounds. "A tetanus shot and a mild sedative should do it," he said.

BLOCKED

The doctor took George to his office while the nurse tended to Ruth.

"Ruth will be fine, George. Just keep her calm for a day or two, and the sedative will help her sleep. You did call the police about this, didn't you?"

"Well, not yet, but I'm sure they'll be involved because we called 911, but then I had to get her out of there. You know how long it can take to get the rescue people up the mountain. I wasn't going to wait around."

"I understand. I'd like for you to tell me what happened."

George settled into the chair that faced the doctor's desk. After a deep sigh, he began.

"It's been festering for a while now. That is to say, I've been worried, but I didn't know what to do."

The doctor looked up from the tablet where he'd written a few notes. "You've been worried, you say? About Ruth?"

"No, not exactly. It's more about Jan Johnson, Doc. You know how we've all felt protective of those two kids. Tried to help them get on here. Be a family for them."

"Oh sure. Jan and Bryce have done well with their art. I've purchased several pieces from them at the Market." He pointed toward the bookcase behind his desk where one of Bryce's boxes was displayed.

George looked out the window for a moment before continuing. "And you know how we were so worried for Bryce. Well, at least Ruth and I were always a little nervous, knowing how they left Atlanta after some troubled times for the boy."

He leaned forward and put one hand on the doctor's desk, as if for support. "But turns out, it's Jan who's having trouble. Kind of makes sense. She's had a heavy load after the parents' sudden death. And lately things have been getting strange. Out of control."

He rubbed his brow vigorously. "I'll start at the beginning, Doc. Jan started coming around to talk with Ruth pretty steady, and it's just continued for a long time. She'd just drop by, and Ruth was getting so attached."

He looked toward the floor for a moment and cleared his throat.

"We never could have children, you see, and so I think Ruth just really took to Jan. Baking cookies and cakes and pies for her. Kind of being a friend and her auntie."

George paused. "Despite everything."

"Despite everything?"

George sank back in the chair. "There's more to this story than you know. And it's not easy to tell."

"Take your time."

"It's been hidden for so long, it's hard to let it out."

"I understand, but anything you tell me is held in confidence, George."

"Thanks, Doc."

George wiped his brow and straightened himself in the chair. "You probably don't know about Ruth having a sister?"

The doctor shook his head.

"Yeah, a sister who was a good bit younger. Angela was her name. Lived in Atlanta after she left home. Never had an easy time, as I understand it. Got into some pretty bad scrapes. Kinda on the wild side. Lots of bad men. Drinking and drugs. That kind of thing. But Ruth, she never gave up on her, and when she got pregnant, from this terrible guy, a criminal hooked on drugs, Ruth went down to Atlanta to stay with her. And she convinced her sister to give up the baby for adoption."

Dr. Davis picked up a small stone that he used for a paperweight. He let its weight and silky finish find a place in his hand. George watched the doctor roll the stone around with his fingers for a few seconds.

"I guess you probably know where I'm going with this story."

"I can guess. But I'm curious about the details. If the baby was given up for adoption, it's not likely that Ruth would know the particulars.

BLOCKED

Adoption agencies keep everything private, as required by law. So, I'm wondering if it was a Grey Market adoption."

"I don't know what it's called, but it wasn't an ordinary adoption. It was what I'd call an under-the-table deal."

"So the Johnsons had the money and clout to get what they wanted, you're saying, without going through regular channels."

"That's right."

"Which means Ruth's sister ended up with a tidy sum of money, or at least enough to pay all of her doctor and hospital bills. That's typical in a Grey Market arrangement."

"I don't know about the money, but as Ruth tells it, her sister went off the deep end after the baby was taken, and she ended up in the psych ward. But they didn't keep her long. She got out and was trying to get Ruth to help her get the baby back. Ruth went along with it for a while because she could see how desperate Angela was. She was afraid Angela would do something crazy."

George slumped forward and rubbed at his eyes.

"And she did, not long after that. She took her own life. Such a terrible thing. The young woman just had too many strikes against her. Grieved my Ruth something awful, though."

The doctor offered the stone to George, and George took it, let it rest in his hand, and then cupped it in both hands.

"It's called a Worry Stone. It's gotten me through some tough moments. Holding it reminds me of the strength we all possess, if we are able to call on it."

George nodded, held it for a moment longer, and handed it back to the doctor. "I might need a whole quarry of those, Doc."

The doctor nodded. "I know what you mean."

"But anyway, Ruth was able to contact the Johnsons, even went to see them. She was meaning to take the baby back, work out something with the Johnsons for the money and all. But when she saw how devoted they were to the baby, she just couldn't bring herself to do anything. I guess she figured the baby had a better chance with them."

"I know that had to be a bad time for Ruth."

George shuddered. "It was hard on both of us. I wanted to comfort her, to help. But there wasn't a thing I could do. Had to just let time do its healing."

"One more question. Did you and Ruth have anything to do with the Johnsons moving here?"

George lowered his head for a moment and picked at a loose thread on his shirtsleeve.

"Not directly. Thing is, while Ruth was in Atlanta with Angela, she met people in the neighborhood. You know how my Ruth loves people and makes friends at the drop of a hat. So she starts going to church there and meeting all kinds of people. When she called me or wrote me her weekly letter, she always had a string of people to tell me about. And even when she gets back home here, she stays in touch, sending cards and letters."

"And that's how she found out about the trouble the Johnsons were having?"

A smile spread across George's face and into his eyes, and pride surged through his voice. "Right, and next thing you know, my Ruth was telling them what a nice community we have here and becoming a one-woman commercial for Hollyville."

The doctor smiled and nodded.

"Just one more question, George. Does Jan know this story?"

"Yes, she does. Ruth had a chance to talk with Jan when Jan finally got around to confiding her fears. See, Jan was real worried when Bryce started looking into his background, and she started fretting over it with

BLOCKED

Ruth. That's when Ruth told me everything. We didn't know what to do, but we decided to stay quiet."

"It's a tangled story, George. Strange how much we don't know about the people around us. We can go for years thinking we know the people and their stories, and then one day, the bottom drops out. You must be feeling terrible about all of this."

"I'm feeling better now, letting the story out. It's been a burden carrying it around, and not knowing what might happen next."

"I'm sure it's been difficult."

"Thing is, Doc, what me and Ruth can't understand. Why did Jan turn on us? Why did she tie up Ruth and start cutting on herself and then on Ruth? It's just pure craziness."

"It's hard to say, George. With all the advancements in medicine, we still know so little about the human mind. Something, perhaps the parents' accident, has made Jan lose contact with reality."

"But she could have lashed out at Bryce or at Lydia Drexel who's taken an interest in her. Why Ruth?"

"It's just a theory, but from what you've told me, it's possible that Jan is rebelling against the mother figures in her life. Eventually, she feels that each of them has let her down in some way, and then to gain control, she looks for a way to fix the problem. Unfortunately, in the process, her mind fails her."

"But Ruth was trying to help her, Doc."

"We both know that, but we cannot expect Jan, when she has lost touch with reality, to act logically or normally."

The doctor placed the stone in its usual resting place and stood up. He came around the desk and when George stood, he put both hands on his friend's shoulders.

"You have the strength to get through this, George. Ruth too. You're both going to be fine. Come and talk with me anytime."

Bryce Visits Lydia

Lydia sat on the porch in one of the rockers, her feet propped up on the railing, a glass of wine in one hand and her cell phone in the other. She hadn't checked in with Charles recently; she had so much to tell him.

"Lyd, darling girl, don't tell me you are still enmeshed in the case of the aging Bobbsey Twins. I was sure you'd have put all of that behind you by now. *Tisk, tisk.* You are not a very good student, are you?"

"No lectures, please, Charles. You know you can't wait to hear what's happened, so just relax and let me fill you in."

"Has some new disaster transpired? It'll have to be good, if it's to top the fire that might have burned down half of North Carolina."

"Dear Charles, King of the Hyperbole."

"Seriously, what's the news you're so eager to spill?"

"Remember the symbols I asked you about? Turns out Jan was the one brandishing them all around, and her latest carving was on her own body—and Ruth's. They're both all right, but the girl snapped. She tied up Ruth and said something about saving everyone from evil. Voices in her head told her to do it."

Charles was silent for a few seconds.

"Jesus, Lydia, what's going on up there?"

"I'm trying to tell you."

"Are you all right?"

"I am, but I have to say that this has not been the simple getaway that you and I envisioned back in May."

BLOCKED

Lydia told Charles about all of the latest happenings.

Talking through it relieved the tension that had built and built without her realizing it. She had known this about herself—that her way of handling things was to meet the crisis head on in perfect calm, but then afterward, to crumble.

The tension in her shoulders would rise until she ached with stiffness. Her head would feel as if it were clamped in a large tourniquet that was being tightened gradually. Mercifully, if she could retell the story to a trusted listener, the pressure would eventually dissipate. Her life would return to normal.

"So I conclude that it was John who saved the day?"

"Yes, he's been wonderful. I really can't say what might have happened if he hadn't arrived when he did."

"Of course we're overlooking the small but significant fact that you could have avoided putting yourself in danger by taking someone with you. Or how about this? You could have called on the police for help. You suspected that the girl had set the fire and yet you went blithely off to see how much more danger you could leap into."

"Charles, calm down. I'm fine."

"*Hmph.*"

"Do you want to hear the story or not?"

Charles let out a long sigh. "Go on."

"Here's the twist. All this time I thought Bryce was the one who had mental or emotional problems, but it was actually Jan. Bryce knew his sister had serious difficulties and was trying to protect everyone from her. But here's the really surprising part. It was Jan's mother who was a rape victim, not Bryce's."

"That *is* a twist."

"I know. No wonder Bryce was acting so peculiarly. Poor kid."

"Come on, Lyd, why didn't Bryce get help if he knew his sister was a threat?"

"Same reason most of us march off on our own thinking we can handle things ourselves."

"Like someone I know?" Charles asked.

Lydia mumbled, "You're right, I did get into something beyond my skills."

"*Again*, shall we add?"

"Don't push it, Charles."

He laughed.

She let out a long sigh and continued, "But probably Bryce was afraid of getting involved with the authorities. They might have made him leave his studio, might have tried to put him under surveillance. I'm sure he was afraid he'd lose all control over his life."

"I'm not sure I buy it. Seems to me he could have found someone to help him. How about you? After all, you've taken a deep interest in both of those kids."

"No, Charles. I'm still just an outsider. You know how these mountain communities are."

"Well, then he could have asked some of the old timers."

Lydia was silent for a moment. "I guess he just couldn't."

"Youthful ignorance."

"No, fear, I think. And wanting to manage it all on his own."

"Okay, whatever. So when are you coming home?"

"Soon, Charles. Soon."

BLOCKED

Not long after this conversation with Charles, Lydia was relaxing, scanning an old issue of *Art in America,* when she recognized the sound of Bryce's truck approaching. It took her by surprise. She wasn't sure where she stood with Bryce. After all, he'd been in the hospital, and now his sister was in the hospital. There hadn't been an opportunity for her to speak with him, and she didn't know what he might have been told.

She poured two glasses of lemonade and went to the porch to wait. She greeted him, invited him to come inside, and handed him the glass.

"You're looking well, Bryce. Have you had any further problems with asthma?"

"I'm fine now."

"I was shocked when I found you passed out on the office floor the day of the fire. At first, I actually feared you were dead."

Bryce nodded. "I guess things would've been a lot different if you and John hadn't arrived when you did."

They were silent for a time, until Bryce picked up the art magazine and began paging through it. Lydia suspected Bryce wanted to talk about Jan and all that had happened, but she decided to wait for him to bring up the topic. She had half expected him to be angry, but he seemed to be unusually calm. "I was reading the article by Dave Hickey. He makes a good case for beauty being in the eye of the beholder, which I strongly believe too."

Bryce looked up, and Lydia sensed his immediate interest.

"The article references the Mapplethorpe incident. Do you know about the explosion over Mapplethorpe's sexually explicit photographs?"

"Yeah, our high school art teacher told us something about it. He thought Mapplethorpe was some kind of pervert. All that did was get most of us charged up about seeing the pictures."

"What did you think of them? Or did you ever get to see them?" Lydia asked.

"Actually, it was kind of over-the-edge. Kind of like that cow dung painting deal that came along a little later. Mr. Snyder went on about that too. Now that I think about it, I guess it was a good way to keep us listening."

Bryce chuckled and Lydia nodded.

"Hickey would argue that we can't censor these artists . . . something about a relationship between democracy and beauty."

Lydia noted Bryce's questioning look.

"You know, it's about the idea of whether the public should be protected from viewing something that isn't perceived to be beautiful. Did your art teacher talk about the stink New York Mayor Giuliani made at the time? He was going to shut down the Brooklyn Museum of Art if they hung the exhibit. But it didn't happen. I went with an artist friend of mine to see the show, probably because we too had to see for ourselves what the fuss was about."

"Well, I don't know, but if we had an exhibit like that here in Hollyville, I can just imagine the kind of shit that would come down."

Lydia laughed. She was pleased that Bryce was relaxed enough to show his sense of humor.

"I like your pun. I wouldn't dream of hanging a show that was spattered with cow or elephant dung, but I want my right to do so to be preserved."

"Do you mind if I borrow this magazine?"

"I'm glad for you to borrow it. In fact, you can keep it."

"Thanks."

Bryce put his glass on the nearby lamp table and turned toward Lydia.

"I wanted to apologize for Jan. I know about everything that went on at the Randolphs. I was worried for a long time that something bad was going to happen."

"I know that, Bryce, and I'm really sorry that you've had this burden to handle all alone. It's been such a difficult thing."

Bryce clamped his hands together and looked at the floor.

Lydia reached out and put her hand on Bryce's shoulder. "A lot of things have become more clear in the past few days. I have to admit that I didn't understand what was happening with Jan—that she was having some kind of breakdown. If I had, I might have made better decisions."

"What do you mean?"

"I think you were right to tell me to mind my own business. I thought I could march in and offer my wisdom and set everything right. You were trying to tell me, but I wasn't listening."

Bryce shook his head repeatedly. "No, no. You wanted to help. That's all."

"Yes, I did, but I let my own needs take over."

Lydia noted the questioning look on Bryce's face.

"I came here to get a fresh look at my work and at myself, but mostly I've become involved in yours and Jan's situation. I meant well, but I used your problems to avoid my own."

Bryce smiled.

BLOCKED

Lydia Talks with George and Ruth

Lydia pulled into the Randolphs' driveway. Ruth had said she felt well enough to have visitors and for Lydia to come for afternoon tea. George met her at the door and welcomed her.

"Come through, this way. She's in the sunroom," George said.

Ruth sat in a wicker chase. Lydia went to her and offered her hand, but Ruth reached up and pulled Lydia to her for a hug.

"Thank you so much for coming to visit me, dear."

"It's so good to see you looking relaxed and well, Ruth. You've had quite a shock."

"I do feel completely recovered, although I suppose I have some work ahead, erasing those troublesome mental images of Jan, you know."

Lydia drew a wicker rocker close to Ruth.

"Thank goodness we were able to get her to the hospital where she can get some help."

"Oh my, yes. I never dreamed that the poor girl was suffering so much. Voices in her head? Just imagine what that must be like, although goodness knows I'm sure we all have some sort of struggle. If you think about it, it's a small wonder that more people don't drop over the edge, if you know what I mean."

"I do know what you mean, and I've often thought the same thing. It's a narrow path between the difficult choices thrown at us."

BLOCKED

"George, dear, would you bring some glasses and the pitcher of tea from the refrigerator? And there's a plate of cookies on the counter."

"Ruth, I don't know if you were aware, but George sprang into action when he arrived. While John and I were trying to decide what to do, George was on the phone calling 911 and then giving us instructions. I was so impressed."

"That's my George. He's always been quick with sorting things out and taking action. But let's not tell him, or he might get a big head." Ruth winked at Lydia.

Lydia accepted the glass of tea and a cookie that George offered and then turned her chair so George could be included in the conversation.

"I can't help remarking on the long struggle you two have endured. It can't have been easy, watching and wondering what might happen with Bryce and Jan."

Lydia saw the look George and Ruth exchanged. They then proceeded to fill her in on the history.

Ruth sighed. "Yes, it's true. I have to tell you that I had mixed feelings when the Johnsons decided to move here. I was both thrilled and terrified at the thought of being able to get close to my niece. At first, of course I saw only the good side, but after the accident, I knew the road ahead would be rocky."

George stood up and walked over to stand beside Ruth. "We toyed with the idea of adopting Jan and Bryce, but we knew there would be too many obstacles. If they had been younger, it might have worked out, but since neither Bryce nor Jan knew their real history, we decided to stay silent."

Lydia wondered if George believed she would be critical of them for their decision. She took comfort, knowing that she was not the only person drawn into the Johnsons' troubles.

"It's always a tough call, determining whether to intervene. I've only recently realized how I allowed myself to be pulled into Jan and Bryce's story, thinking I had simple solutions for them. I see now that I was beyond my depth."

Ruth put her hand out to touch Lydia. "My dear, you were only acting out of the goodness of your heart. Who could fault you for that?"

Lydia smiled and grasped Ruth's hand in both of hers.

"Both of you have acted not only with love, but also with wisdom."

"It's good of you to say that, but we were pretty confused over what to do, weren't we, George?"

"That's right. We kept the family secret when maybe we shouldn't have."

"No one would blame you for that. Certainly, I don't," Lydia said.

Ruth looked at George before turning to Lydia. "We know Jan will need long-term help."

"That's right, but it's totally possible for her to have a normal life with therapy and medication. It's good that she will have your love and support."

George nodded. "She can live with us when she's released from the hospital."

Ruth reached for her husband's hand. "Oh yes, I think that would be the right thing to do. And as her aunt, I can be her guardian. Isn't that right?"

Lydia said, "I'm not sure of the legal aspects of a case like this, but I think Jan may welcome the chance to be free from the responsibility she has felt since her adoptive parents' death. I hope that after a time, she may be able to go to college. You may know that she has spoken about becoming a teacher."

"That is a dream I've had for our dear Jan for a long time."

George laughed. "Now, don't you two get too busy making all of Jan's decisions for her."

Ruth smiled at her husband. "I told Lydia while you were out of the room that you're the one who always knows how to solve problems and to lead."

"No, not at all, but I do know young people have to have space and chances to make mistakes."

"See how wise he is," Ruth said.

Lydia nodded, looking toward George. "What do you think will happen to Bryce now?"

"Bryce is capable of staying here and running his studio. There's more than enough money for him to do that, according to my friend who manages their estate."

Lydia shook her head. "Oh, I know it sounds as if I'm making decisions for him, but I see how talented and how bright he is. I hope he'll have a chance to study and to travel—to be exposed to more of the world."

"Time will tell," George said.

Lydia and John Discuss their Future

Twilight had always been one of Lydia's favorite times. Seeing the way the light played with the darkness, creating new shapes and unusual shadows, all of it fascinated her. She also remembered her mother's love for this time of the day when the work was done, and the family gathered under the large maple tree in lawn chairs to relax and let the southerly breezes flow over them on a summer evening.

Here in the mountains, the chilled air brought a shiver that sent Lydia inside for her sweater and a cup of hot tea. She returned to her favorite spot on the porch railing where she could see the fireflies dotting the gradually darkening space around the cabin, hear the whip-poor-wills' cries, and feel the dampness of the air seep into her skin.

Her thoughts turned to the chain of events that had cascaded down and around her in the past week. At last, she felt a leveling of the pressure that had possessed her. For the first time in days, her head was clear without even a hint of ache. Her shoulders and limbs were free from tension. She felt normal again, but normal meant back to Square One—the purpose for her trip. Aside from knowing that she wanted a break from her job, she was unsure of what exactly lay ahead.

What a coincidence. She smiled as she heard John's truck making the climb toward the cabin. Warmth flowed through her mind and body.

When the truck door slammed, Lydia put her cup down on the railing and went down the steep path to meet him.

"Oh John, I'm so glad to see you."

He pulled her into his arms, held her firmly, and whispered into her hair. "I had to be with you this evening."

His kiss thrilled her even more than the first time.

They climbed the path together, holding hands, and she said, "Come inside."

Lydia opened a bottle of Pinot Noir and set it and two glasses on the coffee table. John poured the wine for them and turned to face Lydia.

"What shall our toast be?"

"To us?"

"Certainly, but what would you like to add?" John asked.

"How about this? A salute to our survival of the Bobbsey Twins."

John laughed. "Excellent!"

He stretched his legs out, sank back into the pile of pillows on the couch, and let one arm slip around Lydia's shoulders.

"It *is* rather funny to think how much drama played out around those two. I feel as if I've been living in a soap opera this past week. You could have died in the fire or been killed with Jan's knife."

"You're right. Either of those things could have happened if you hadn't come to help."

Lydia cuddled against John and sighed in contentment.

For those few moments, they each savored the feeling of comfort.

Lydia sat up straight and looked into John's eyes. "I've been thinking about what I want to do."

John gave her a questioning look. "And?"

"I think I want to take a semester's absence from my job."

He waited for more.

"I need it for several reasons. One, I'm physically exhausted after this supposed rest. Two, I'm totally without inspiration for painting, although I do feel it will return at any moment now, which means I could get a large block of work done on a leave. And three, I want to spend more time with you. If you're here and I'm there, I know we wouldn't have enough time together."

"Spoken like a true academic."

Lydia swatted him playfully. "Cut that out, or I may have to find some labels for you."

"Oh, and what might those be?"

Lydia giggled. "How about 'my hero' and 'divine kisser,' for starters?"

John grabbed her and kissed her with such fervor that they ended up in the bedroom for the next half hour.

They lay there in the tangle of sheets so relaxed that they were almost drifting into sleep. Suddenly John turned to Lydia and took her face between his hands so that he could look into her eyes.

"I think this means we should get married. What do you think?"

Lydia feigned boredom with a yawn and a light peck on John's cheek. But when she saw the distressed look in his eyes, she quickly amended her response. She drawled, "Well, we might take your proposal under advisement, but . . ."

"But what?"

"I'll soon have lived fifty-one years on this earth, and at this time in my life, I expect—as I've been dropping hints for some time now—a properly romantic proposal."

"Hmm. I suppose I could take *that* proposal under advisement," he teased.

"Right. Why don't you do that?"

John tickled her until she giggled, but then she took the initiative, kissing him deeply and stroking him until they were enthralled in their passion once again.

BLOCKED

After a short nap, Lydia went to the living room to fetch the wine and their glasses.

"I think we should meet tomorrow on the hiking trail for a re-enactment of how and when this all began."

"Fantastic. And don't be surprised if you get a wedding proposal worthy of a movie production."

"So be it and amen."

"Is that a hint that you want a church wedding?"

"Possibly. We have a beautiful chapel at Spring Valley, but I wouldn't be opposed to an outdoor wedding, if we can prepare for a weather glitch."

First John laughed, and soon Lydia joined in. When they'd finally stopped, she asked, "What?"

He pulled her to him and whispered in her hair. "Do you think we could hold off on the wedding plans until I've had a chance to plan my super romantic proposal?"

Lydia pulled away and put her hands over her face. "Oh great Scott, you're right. What am I doing, jumping ahead?"

"No, no, no. Believe me, Lyd, I want you to always tell me exactly what you want. It's absolutely the best way to make a marriage work."

"You won't think I'm too controlling?"

"I most certainly may think you are too controlling, but remember this. We can always talk it over and out until we find a way to make things work."

"Oh John, I really do love you."

"I know. And we're going to be wonderful together because we already are. Don't ever forget that." He brought her to him in a loving, secure embrace. "You are my only love for the rest of my life."

John went home feeling elated and yet calm. He had the wonderful task of planning what he hoped would be a memorable time for his Lydia.

Scrap met him at the door.

"Hello there, Scrap. Are you ready for this news? You and I are going to the office to plan a romantic proposal. But first, I know you want a snack and your brushing, both of which you shall have."

Content, Scrap sat curled up on a corner of the office desk where John doodled on a pad. His mind had shot ahead to the outdoor wedding. How could he avoid that weather glitch Lydia had forecasted?

Soon, a drawing of a flower-laden arbor for the wedding party took shape. He could use branches of rhododendron over a lattice roof and frame the front opening with cut flowers woven into a mesh frame. Streamers of ribbons could be attached intermittently in colors Lydia wanted.

He knew a perfect spot for their outdoor wedding ceremony.

☙

The day was clear and cool, perfect weather for their outing. John chose a comfortable but attractive shirt and tight-fitting jeans, an outfit he knew Lydia liked. Next, he filled a cooler with a bottle of white wine and fresh strawberries and watermelon slices. In a basket, he put two elegant wine glasses and two kinds of cheese with a loaf of wheat berry bread that he knew Lydia favored. As an extra treat, he selected a bar of dark chocolate laced with almonds and orange bits, another of Lydia's favorites.

They met at the same trailhead at the same time as they had on their first date. Lydia arrived only a few minutes after John.

She teased him with a reference to the exchange they'd had three months ago. "I see you're a little early. You're *still* eager?"

"You bet. Eager and ready." He took her in his arms and kissed her hello.

※

Twenty minutes into their hike, they came to the lookout where they had first met. John and his nephew Josh had been resting there when Lydia came along.

"Oh, just look at that view. It's even more beautiful than I remembered," Lydia said. "I know it's a cliché, but it literally takes my breath away."

They stood letting their gaze take in the beauty. Because it was an unusually clear day, they could see for miles into what brochures claimed was the intersection of three states: North and South Carolina and Tennessee.

"And *you* take my breath away, my darling Lydia." He took her hand and pulled her along to the rock slab that formed a resting place.

"Sit here with me, and we'll have some wine and fruit, but first I want to ask you something."

He bent on one knee, looked into Lydia's eyes, and said, "You mean more to me than all that we see before us. You are more beautiful than these mountains, more intelligent and gracious than the years represented in the earth that surrounds us, more loving and nurturing than time itself. And you make me believe that together we can build a world that will survive pain and suffering. Stay with me, dearest Lydia, forever as my bride—my wife."

"Oh John, that's so beautiful." She brushed tears from her eyes, and he offered her his handkerchief.

"Well?"

"Yes, oh most definitely, yes!"

He reached into his pocket and withdrew a ring. "This ring was my grandmother's ring, and it's always had a special place in my heart. Would you honor me by wearing it, dear Lydia?"

John slipped the ring with its double row of small, delicate diamonds onto Lydia's finger and pulled her to her feet so he could embrace her.

Again, he wiped away her tears.

"Now sit down. I want to show you something." He pulled his sketches from his back pocket. "This is what Scrap and I worked on last night after I left you."

She opened the sheets of paper carefully.

"This is my solution to weather problems for that outdoor wedding you want."

"Oh, it is so beautiful. It's perfect."

"And I know the perfect place for it. I'll take you there, and we'll see if you agree."

Lydia Makes Plans

Over her morning coffee, Lydia reviewed her plans: She would go back to the campus to hand in the paperwork for a leave of absence. She would recommend a friend of hers who could fill in for her, a former student who was without a job at the moment. Her house, she could rent to her friend, which would solve a passel of problems. One major item pleased her especially: It wouldn't be necessary to empty her house, but some minor adjustments would have to be made. The guest room could serve her renter as a bedroom, but it would need an Internet connection. It would not be smart to turn over her office and her computer to a renter, no matter how reliable she might be.

Her mind leaped ahead to the wedding. She and John had agreed to keep their wedding party small; only their closest friends and family would be included. But just as soon as they began drafting the list, they saw how challenging it was to limit. In the end, they'd decided that the friends they'd made in Hollyville should be invited too. Lydia hoped Jan and Bryce, as well as Ruth and George would attend. Jan might be permitted to have the day away from the hospital if she were under the Randolphs' care.

They wanted to have the wedding while the weather was more likely to cooperate and had set the date for Sunday of Labor Day weekend when it would be easier for traveling friends to get away.

With only a few weeks left, Lydia felt both zany and euphoric. There were colors and dresses and flowers and caterers to consider. Her newest mantra had become, "Keep it simple." But with each new decision, it seemed another layer of complexity was added.

Lydia was stunned and gratified when John asked if she thought Charles might like to give her away. Such a sensitive man. She toyed with the idea of asking Jan to be her maid of honor, but she could hear Charles's strident voice: "Dear girl, have you lost all of your sense?" Instead, she would ask Ruth to be her matron of honor, and John had already chosen George as the best man. These were the people who had helped bring them closer together in recent weeks.

※

Back at the campus, Lydia met with her department chair, Richard Simpson.

"To be perfectly frank, I was quite surprised to receive your application for a leave of absence. If you don't mind, I'd like to know what has brought this on. Of course, we have people who are ill or they have other unusual circumstances that require them to have time away immediately, but from all I can tell, this is a sudden decision on your part. I'd like to know if there is some problem with the department or your job, Dr. Drexel."

Lydia couldn't help laughing.

Her department chair pulled himself up in his large office chair to a rigid position and all but pointed a finger at Lydia. "This is a serious situation, I want you to know. Most certainly, it is not a laughing matter. You've put me in a delicate spot, requiring me to put in extra hours to bring everything properly in line for the department, the school, and your temporary replacement."

Lydia stifled her laugh. She had never been a fan of Richard Simpson, who managed to take himself far too seriously. She rather enjoyed putting him in a spot.

"It's nothing like that, Dr. Simpson. Actually, it's wonderfully happy news. I'm getting married."

Simpson did a double take and dropped the file folder he had been looking at, sending the papers to the floor.

"Getting married? Surely not. Does this mean you'll be leaving us permanently? I thought you only wanted a semester's leave. So actually you're taking a leave so you can look for another job. That's it, isn't it?"

Lydia thought how much fun it would be to string him along, letting him believe an unlimited amount of extra work lay ahead of him. Instead she stooped to pick up the papers nearest her and handed them to the overweight man who was struggling to reach the scattered papers at his feet.

Lydia stood facing Simpson, letting him know that she was finished with this interview. "My fiancée and I have not made long-range plans. I only know that I need some time off to do my painting and to enjoy my husband."

"But, but, but," Simpson sputtered. "I can't function as chair if I don't know what your plans are."

"My plans are to take this fall semester off, to paint every day, and to enjoy my marriage. I will be in touch with you about any additional plans. Meanwhile, I recommend Amanda James for the position while I'm gone. She was a student of mine years ago, and I can vouch for her abilities as a teacher as well as an artist. She can rent my house while I'm away, which will make things easy all around. Of course, if you'd rather find my replacement yourself?" Lydia left the question hanging.

"No, no, no. Amanda James. I seem to remember the name."

"It's not surprising as she was one of our best. We're lucky that she is currently between jobs and can take this position. And here's another suggestion. If you haven't found a person to fill in for Charles Harris, you may be able to kill two birds with one stone, so to speak. Possibly, Amanda could arrange to fill that position second semester.

Lydia walked toward the door and turned to face Simpson, who had strained to stand. "Thank you for your time, Dr. Simpson. I'll be in touch."

She felt a smile filling her face and then her entire body. It felt remarkably good to have the upper hand for a few moments, especially with a difficult person like Simpson. She could hardly wait to tell Charles about her good fortune.

༶

Charles was in his office grading papers for a quiz he had given in Art History 101 that morning when Lydia knocked on his door.

"You're back? Why, you little scamp, the very idea of not letting me know."

"But Charles you always told me you love surprises, as long as they're good. Are you saying I'm not a good surprise?"

They laughed as she strode toward him. He gave her his usual Charles hug, not too short and not too long.

"Sit down and tell me everything, dear girl. Do."

Lydia slipped into the easy chair opposite Charles's desk. "I just came from Simpson's office where I had a wonderful time giving him grief."

Charles let out a belly laugh. "How delicious. The man has become more and more difficult. He deserves anything you were able to throw at him. But let's not waste time on him. You, dear girl, are absolutely glowing. I gather that you and John are rolling full tilt toward marriage. What's the latest?"

"So glad you asked. You're right. We're making our wedding plans, and I have a special request for you."

"Fire away. I'll do whatever I can to make your special day a happy occasion. But let it be known, if you're thinking of leaving your job permanently, I'll initiate a full-scale rebellion."

Lydia laughed. She loved his sense of drama. "Because you are such a dear friend, I'd like for you to give me away."

For a moment, she thought Charles would cry. He recovered nicely and came from behind his desk to give her an extra hug.

"This calls for a special celebration. What say we go to our favorite bar for a proper toast?"

While they walked the few blocks, Charles told Lydia about the student researcher, Bruce Hanson, who had become an "absolute Godsend."

"The lad has remarkable writing skills. And you can surely imagine how I revel in the fact that I don't have to teach him documentation skills. How I wish we could get our English Department to take their jobs more seriously."

"Now Charles, maybe in this case, 'the lad,' to borrow your term, is simply an independent thinker and doer. No need to blame the English Department."

"*Hmph.* Seems I recall your slinging some arrows in that direction. Has being in love taken away your zeal for abuse?"

Lydia laughed. "Listen, Charles. There were times this summer when I could have slung whole bags of abuse in your direction. A happy little getaway. Indeed. Instead, I nearly lost my life several times."

"Well now, Lyd dear, you know you can't properly hang that on me because guess who went looking for all the scrapes she could get herself into?"

"Actually, you are right. I've come to see, maybe more clearly than ever before, how easily I avoid my own problems by taking on those of others."

"Here, here. So what is your solution for your future? And I don't mean concerning problem-solving."

"You mean future career plans? I've told John that I want to take this leave to sort things out a bit more and to paint, paint, paint. As soon as we are settled properly into our marriage, I think I'll be ready to resume my work here. I can't imagine giving up teaching."

"Is it going to be one of those new long-distance arrangements with you here and John in the mountains?"

"We haven't quite sorted that out, but John says he can do his construction work anywhere, so maybe he'll set up here. He already works some in Asheville."

"Maybe he'll build you that dream studio you've yearned for."

"What a splendid idea, Charles!"

"And maybe you'll be ready to come to Italy next spring while I'm there."

"Another exceptional plan!"

"Well, well, darling girl. I do believe we've solved the most immediate problems."

Charles lifted his glass. "Here's to a long life of happiness here and abroad."

Lydia's Painting

Lydia's new paintings would open in a solo show in Asheville at the end of the month. As usual, there were a thousand details to take care of, but she didn't mind. How could she mind when only a few months ago she had been afraid she would never find a new idea for her work?

She stood in front of her easel, admiring her favorite painting, searching for the best title. This was the painting she considered to be her "breakthrough" piece.

Intense colors boiled forth on the canvas—brilliant reds and oranges and yellows, surrounding a black hole. Beyond the swirling colors lay a background of serene blue, green, and white. It was a palette totally different than what she would have normally chosen.

When she began the painting, she'd felt driven to expunge herself from the feelings that had held her in bondage. She had let the brush float over the surface, almost without a sense of direction. Nothing like what she would have painted six months or a year ago, its process fascinated her. It wasn't that she'd left all of her formal instruction behind, although she anticipated that her colleagues might argue that point. It was more that she had allowed herself to experiment and explore, to work solely from her feelings.

It had been liberating. Thrilling. Fulfilling.

She knew she had been released.

"Released." She reached for a pencil, and on the back of the painting's stretcher, wrote the title.

BLOCKED

Satisfied, she went to her computer to record the title for her upcoming show. This was the painting she would use for her publicity, the painting she would showcase.

She walked around the studio where she had placed the other new canvases, double-checking her selection, reviewing each painting one more time. All of it felt right. Not just the placement of the paintings, and not just the sizes and the frames. It was so much more than that. It was the feeling the work commanded. She knew the work was good. Better than good. It was some of the best she had ever done.

Thoughts rolled through her mind. So much had happened since those months when her painting had come to a standstill, when she had felt her creativity was forever blocked.

John had come into her life. Dear, wonderful John. How she loved him.

Jan and Bryce. Such trauma had surrounded them, but some of the shadows were lifting, especially under the loving care of George and Ruth. Even though she had gotten too involved in their problems, she would never regret that strange interlude. It had forced her to understand more about herself and others.

The Wedding

Lydia slept late the morning of her wedding. She lay in her bed admiring the engagement ring John had placed on her finger. Its grace and elegance pleased her. In all of her imaginings, she had not included a ring. It was not a requirement, despite her wish—John would say her *demand*—for a romantic proposal. She smiled; she loved the fact that John had the confidence to confront her with her foibles. But even more, she admired his statement that they would always be able to talk out their problems and to settle their differences. She knew that this was, just as John had said, the basis for a successful marriage.

She glanced at her wedding gown, hanging on the closet door in its plastic bag. She could admire its elegance from where she sat against a stack of pillows in her bed. Ribbons and lace. She hadn't thought she would be that kind of bride, but when she'd gone shopping, the only gown that had caught her attention was this one with its yards and yards of off-white cotton. And when she'd put it on, it had fit her as if it had been hand-tailored for her.

The plunging neckline had put her off at first, but when she saw how it complemented her figure, she knew it was the right choice.

She stepped into the steaming scented bath and allowed herself to sink into its bubbles with abandonment. *My last hours as a single woman. And not a single hint of remorse.*

BLOCKED

The wedding was set for 7:00 p.m. in the park, at the edge of Hollyville. Part of a parcel of land preserved by the Nature Conservancy, it presented a feeling of holiness with its untouched woodlands. Shafts of sunlight fell against the trees and undergrowth, creating lacy patterns. All was quiet. Only the low sounds of nature intervened.

In the clearing, folding chairs sat in semicircular rows, forming an outdoor theater for the wedding. John and his workmen had fashioned the arbor from the sketch he'd shown Lydia when he proposed. Bows of greens covered the wood frame, and flowers and ribbons in a rainbow of colors dressed the opening where the couple would stand to exchange their vows. Designed for its beauty and for protection against rain, it would not be challenged. It was a perfect evening.

Charles extended his arm to Lydia. She smiled at him, and they began their walk toward the bower.

John in his dark blue suit waited for his approaching bride.

Lydia would always remember the look on his face, a look of love and pride.

The simple, traditional vows were exchanged and when the couple turned to greet their friends and wellwishers, Lydia let her eyes scan the small group. A few of her colleagues from the college were there, and in the front row, Jan and Bryce.

Lydia looked at John and said, "Perfect. That's what our wedding is. Perfect."

About the Author

Joanna Innes grew up on a Missouri farm. She graduated from Central Methodist University, Fayette, Missouri, in 1959 with a teaching degree in English. In that same year, she married her artist husband James Innes who encouraged her to become a writer.

After teaching language arts in the public schools for many years, she earned an MA in Composition and Linguistics from Indiana University of PA. From 1989 until her retirement in 2003, she taught courses in freshman composition and directed the writing center at Newberry College, Newberry, SC.

A widow for the past seven years, Innes resides with her precocious cat Ava in Charleston, SC, where she enjoys the supportive atmosphere for writers. She belongs to two writing groups and has participated in numerous courses and workshops. Her other interests include travel, tennis, and playing clarinet and recorder in two established groups.

Made in the USA
Middletown, DE
19 August 2017